I0672704

SWEET CHEAT

SWEET CHEAT

PETER DUNCAN

CUTTING EDGE

Copyright © 1959 by Lurton Blassingame

The characters and events portrayed in this book are fictitious. Any similarity
to real persons, living or dead, is coincidental and not intended by the author.
No part of this book may be reproduced, or stored in a retrieval system,
or transmitted in any form or by any means, electronic, mechanical,
photocopying, recording, or otherwise, without express written permission
of the publisher.

ISBN-13: 978-1-957868-22-6

Published by
Cutting Edge Books
PO Box 8212
Calabasas, CA 91372
www.cuttingedgebooks.com

CHAPTER ONE

GUESS some policemen can feel it in their bones when a day is going to bring murder with it, but I couldn't, so, all unsuspecting, I got up at nine o'clock on what was to be the unholiest Sunday morning in Greenhill history and had breakfast with Mama. That was my first mistake.

She's a big, godly, white-haired, river-raised woman and looks something like Robert E. Lee—without the beard, of course—but she goes at a question like a crawfish. A crawfish moves backward and that's the way she asks questions. She gives you the answer, then she asks you the question.

"Buck," she said, "that was your shirt crammed way down in the hamper, wasn't it?"

See what I mean? Papa had been dead ten years and there hadn't been any burglars undressing in the house, so naturally it was my shirt crammed down in the hamper.

"Yes'm," I said.

"Then you had another tussle with them girls down at Alma's café didn't you? I never saw so much lipstick!"

Well, I was a deacon at First Church and was due to usher in an hour, but the only merciful thing to do was to lie about that lipstick. So I told her that she was right, that the boys had had their usual Saturday night knuckle bee down at Alma's and I had stopped by and quieted them down. "One of the girls was right drunk," I said, "and mistook me for somebody else and threw herself around my neck."

That's when she really started in with her crawfishing questions. "Buck," she said, "you're twenty-eight years old and you're six-foot-three and weigh around two hundred pounds, don't you?"

"Yes'm," I sighed.

"And you played football and you were one of them All-Americans and you were a big hero in Korea, weren't you?"

I'd played football but I hadn't really been any hero. Some Chinamen got me and some other fellows hemmed in a couple of times and I got some medals for getting us unhemmed.

"Yes'm," I said.

"And, if you ever forgot that you were a deacon and a chief of police, you could whip any five men in town, couldn't you?"

"I doubt it," I said.

"Well, they used to say that Lint Bodine could whip any four men in town, didn't they, and you whipped him so bad it took two doctors and a blacksmith to put him back together, didn't it?"

Lint was a bully and I had got out of patience with him about beating his wife, but he wasn't too much of a fighter because he couldn't stand to hear bones snap or see blood in any quantity. The blacksmith had to make a brace for his neck because his head was left a little out of line.

"Yes'm," I said.

"Well," she said, "if Lint Bodine and all them Chinamen couldn't push you around then how come you have so much trouble with them wormy little girls at Alma's?"

Like I say, I hadn't got that lipstick at Alma's, but it would've broke Mama's heart if I'd told her where I had got it so I told her another lie.

"Because," I said, "Lint and them Chinamen weren't drunk but that girl was and there ain't anything as shifty as a girl full of Alma's whisky."

"Well," she sighed, "it's a shame but I'm mighty glad to know it was in line of duty. That's mighty delicate lipstick on that shirt and I was afraid you might've been carrying on with some nice girl."

That called for another lie because it was a nice girl's lipstick and I'd been carrying on with her for twelve years but only because I loved her and was bound by a sacred oath to serve her in all ways, both body and soul. So I sighed and told Mama that she knew better than to think I'd carry on with a nice girl and she sighed and said, sure, that if ever there was a Christian boy it was me.

So I finished breakfast and kissed Mama good-by and told her to stop bothering about my shirts and then I went down to the City Hall to check on the happenings of the night. Greenhill is a river town and is just about what the name says. It sits on this big sloping hill in a bend in the river. It hasn't got but around ten thousand people in it, including Mill Town, and that's why the police station and the jail are in the City Hall.

Chastain Chambers had been on Saturday night duty and he was sitting out front on one of the benches when I got there. He's a tall, flashy, black-haired, sweet-smelling fellow with little gray eyes and big green tongue from drinking on duty and trying to hide it with mints. In short, he wasn't the pride of the force. Kip Belton, the Police Commissioner on the City Council, had hired him, not me.

But I was always pleasant to him and, in a smirking sort of way, he was always pleasant to me. When I asked him if there had been any trouble during the night he said, nope, things had been pretty quiet.

"Of course," he said, "they had that Stag Night out at the Country Club and a bunch of fellows went out to Rita Singleton's afterward and Kip had to go out and quiet them down, but outside of that everything was fine."

Then he sort of smirked and said, "Kip came by here around eleven o'clock after that fracas, hunting for you, but I told him you was out on the river fishing as usual. That got him pretty mad but outside of that nothing happened at all."

Well, that got me pretty mad too, because a Police Commissioner in a little town like Greenhill ain't got any more business going around personally enforcing the law than the Water Works Commissioner has going around personally turning folks' water off. But I didn't say anything. I just thanked Chastain for his vigilance and told him to tell Delbert Tate that I would be by after church to see him. Delbert was the Assistant Chief of Police and hand-chose by me and if he knew anything about the fracas at Rita's I could get the truth from him.

Then I went on out Main Street to my church. It's a real pretty cream-colored stone church with columns. You go up these big steps and instead of entering through a center door there's vestibules on either side. Two ushers stand out in the vestibules and when people come in they usher them to their pews.

Well, mine was the right-hand vestibule and, as soon as I stepped inside, I was face to face with the man who was always causing me grief on Sundays—Mayor Johnson Phelps, who didn't have any more business being a deacon and an usher than Chastain did a policeman. He's a big white-haired fellow about sixty and looks something like W. C. Fields, but on account of his position and money nobody ever mentions it to him. Well, he lit on me like he hadn't seen me in twenty years and unfortunately there wasn't anybody in the vestibule to temper his greeting.

"Well, if it ain't my dear friend in Jesus, Buckingham Peters, Jr.," he said, throwing his arms around me. "My, but you do look godly this morning, son!"

Naturally he knew how such sacrilegious talk offended me and how I hated having him call me son, but he kept right on with it until some of the elderly ladies of the church started coming in and making over me as usual. Miss Nellie Heath said I got handsomer every day and how nice it was to have such a fine boy setting an example for the young people of the town, and Miss

Lucy Adams said about the same thing and whispered that she was baking a lemon cheese cake for me.

And that's the way it went for about fifteen minutes and Mr. Phelps just stood by and grinned like I was putting something over on the old ladies. Then Miss Hattie Ebersole came in and he started doing an imitation of me. He put on a long face and took her hand like he was almost going to kiss it and then he said real doleful, "Hattie, my dear, how are you? How's dear George?"

Miss Hattie looked at him like he was one of the Twelve Disciples and said George wasn't doing a bit better. Mr. Phelps shook his head real sad and told her not to worry though. "He'll whip that thing yet, Hattie. Dear, there's not a night I don't mention him in my prayers."

Miss Hattie squeezed his hand and thanked him and said he was such a good man and then he ushered her down to her pew. It made me almost sick, knowing how he was laughing inside. George was Miss Hattie's drinking brother and had a liver like a goose and Mr. Phelps really didn't feel sorry for him at all. He said anybody who'd drink martinis ought to die.

Well, while I was watching him, I got a whiff of perfume and all of a sudden it wasn't a holy Sunday morning any more, it was a sinful summer night and I was lying in a beautiful garden with a beautiful girl lying right alongside me. I turned around and there the beautiful girl was—Lacey Belton, Kip Belton's wife. She was with Pert Belton, Kip's eighteen-year-old sister. When my eyes met Lacey's I felt like I always did, like she had unscrewed my head and was pumping live steam into my veins. She was the nice girl who had got the lipstick on my shirt the night before.

She was twenty-eight years old, just my age, and was tall and blond and so proud and beautiful looking that she could have been one of those Greek goddesses that made men burn incense and tear the hearts out of sheep. I had loved her since I was sixteen and she had loved me and I guessed we would go on loving one another until the fires of hell claimed our scarlet souls or the Lord showed us the mercy he had showed David and Bathsheba.

She barely spoke, which was our way, but I had my usual trouble with Pert. She wasn't but eighteen but she had soft, shiny, black hair, big warm, devilish blue eyes, lips as red and full as ripe plums and a body that bounced and wiggled so that she looked like she had been stuffed with jelly and snakes.

And naturally what made it so bad was that she knew how good looking and distracting she was and she just loved to run you crazy. Especially me, because I was the one man in town who didn't want to have anything to do with her. Which meant that she did more cooing and swishing and deep breathing and flaunting around me than anybody.

And that's what she did this time. She grabbed my hand and gave it a squeeze and looked up at me like we were in a bedroom instead of a vestibule and said, "Hi, Yum-Yum," which was one of her pet names for me. Now usually she would make just one remark like that and go on, but this time she kept holding on to my hand and looked at Lacey with this strange gleam in her eye and asked her if it would be all right if she stayed behind so we could neck for a while.

She loved to do that sort of thing because she was jealous of Lacey. Everybody said that they were the two best-looking girls in town which didn't make any difference to Lacey but it did to Pert. She wanted to be the only peacock in the barnyard and whenever there was a man around she would always act like he was paying more attention to her than Lacey. Well, as usual Lacey just gave her that cold, glittering look of hers and I jerked my hand loose and ushered them down toward the Belton pew.

Just about every man in the congregation turned to stare and when I passed Mr. Phelps in the aisle he gave me a wink and I knew he would have something nasty to say when I got back to the vestibule and sure enough he did.

"Buck," he drooled, peering down at Lacey, "I own the Johnson cotton mill, three, big farms, two blocks of buildings and..."

I stopped him right there. When I had been going with Lacey in high school and college you couldn't have paid a man to say anything about her to me because I had once knocked out five of a fellow's teeth for doing so, but when she married Kip they figured they would be lusting after his wife instead of my girl and that I wouldn't have any objections.

I still had objections but I couldn't raise an outcry or hit anybody because then there would be talk that I was in love with another man's wife, so all I could do was just object on general principles. So I said, "Mr. Phelps, I know exactly what you're going to say about Lacey because you say it every Sunday and I just ain't interested."

That didn't stop him though. "No, you don't know what I'm going to say," he said, "because I've changed my mind. Last Sunday I said I wouldn't give anything but my cotton mill and two of my farms to bed Lacey down but this morning I would throw in all my buildings, all my Coca Cola stock, all my..."

"Mr. Phelps," I said, "you ought to be ashamed of yourself."

"Oh, no," he said, "you ought to be ashamed of yourself because you were the one who made her so cold and Christian with all that Young People's Christian Union junk you stuffed in her head."

He was referring to mine and Lacey's high school days when we were the head of the young people's activities at the church and all the mothers and fathers in town were making the mistake of wishing their sons and daughters were as Christian as we were.

"As for that pretty little Pert," Mr. Phelps said, "I would throw in my wife, five thousand shares of Chase Manhattan and..."

"Mr. Phelps," I said, "if you keep talking that way I am going over into the other vestibule."

He just laughed and grabbed my arm and gave it a squeeze and said that I wouldn't dream of leaving the one real, understanding friend I had in the world. That was supposed to be him.

"You see all those people in that congregation, Buck?" he said. "They don't understand you. They think you're just a nice, big, lovable chump. I don't. I'm your friend. I understand you. I know you for what you are, a crafty, time-abiding, conniving, blackmailing fiend!"

Now as the Chief of Police of Greenhill I could have arrested him for slander and disturbing public worship but I didn't because I felt sorry for him just like I feel sorry for everybody who is bitter at heart and who's been found out.

I had found Mr. Phelps out when I was just a boy of eighteen or so. At that time he was known as the best duck-hunter and fisherman on the whole river, even though he hadn't been at it more than five years. He always brought back duck or fish and I envied him his skill more than I did his money.

We were still living on the river then and one real bad day in January I saw him heading downstream in his duck boat and I decided to sneak along after him and see if I could learn some of his secrets about hunting. I hadn't followed him more than a mile when I knew something mighty strange was going on. He kept flushing blacks and greenheads out of the willows and had all sorts of good shots but he never paid them any mind at all.

About ten miles down the river he turned into Harney's Creek and I sneaked in after him. Then about two miles up the creek things got even stranger. I found his boat hitched to a dock that served a lodge that a rich man from Jackson was supposed to own. I hove to out of sight in the willows and waited, figuring that maybe he and the rich fellow were going duck-hunting together, but then I saw a big, fancy car coming down the road to the lodge and when it pulled up in front a real fancy, young blond girl got out and went in.

Well, I thought he was going duck-hunting with her, even though she didn't seem exactly the duck-hunting type. But after a half hour, when they didn't come out, I thought maybe she had come to rob him so I sneaked up to the lodge and peeked in a window they had left ajar.

It was the most degrading spectacle I ever saw. Mr. Phelps was stark naked except for his duck-hunting cap and he was lying cross ways on a big wide bed blowing his duck call at the girl. She didn't even have a cap on. She was stark naked, too, and waddling around the room quacking and shaking and acting like a duck.

Every time that Mr. Phelps blew the duck call, she would waddle in closer to the bed like he was decoying her in. Then he would make a grab for her and she would laugh and quack real loud and waddle out of his reach. Finally he grabbed her and she couldn't get loose.

She quacked something frantic and laughed and tried to fight him off but he grabbed her around the waist and yanked her on the bed.

It was a mighty sinful sight, and I ought to have left but I was worried that Mr. Phelps might have a heart attack or that girl might drive him out of his mind and either way he would need somebody to get him home.

But pretty soon it was all over and the girl gave Mr. Phelps a little pat and got up and lit a cigarette and fixed them both a drink and then got back in bed and Mr. Phelps started talking.

He sounded pretty sad and said he didn't like to do such things but his wife drove him to it. He said when they first got married they had fun every night and sometimes before break-fast and always on Sunday afternoons. The next year, though, it was just three times a week and the next year not even that and then she started having them bed-time headaches and before he knew it she had cut him down to fifteen minutes on Sunday evening, and not even then if there was something good on the radio.

He said it was bad enough being sandwiched in between Charlie McCarthy and Manhattan Merry-Go-Round but what really burned him up was her calling him a sex maniac and saying it was all he ever thought about. How could a man keep from thinking about it, he said, when he had been cut down to once a week and then like his wife was feeding the dog.

He said that was what drove him to buying the lodge and taking up fishing and duck-hunting. It was either that or go bankrupt. He just couldn't run a business when he was thinking about sex all the time. A good duck-hunt always cleared his mind, though, so that he could run his business and make money and buy his wife all the things she wanted. In other words, he was doing what he was doing just out of love for her.

Well, the girl in bed with him said, sure, and then she got playful and pretty soon Mr. Phelps got to grinning and got up and took another big drink and then *he* started quacking and waddling around like a duck and the girl started blowing the call. Now that really was revolting and I had to force myself to stay there and watch—which was a real bad mistake because just as the girl grabbed Mr. Phelps I heard these footsteps behind me.

As soon as I heard them I whirled around and there was this big, mean-looking fellow turning the corner of the lodge. He had a shotgun in one hand and a bunch of ducks in the other. I'd never seen him before but I knew from hearsay that he was Gumbo Smith, the caretaker of the lodge, and that he had killed a man once for trespassing.

Well, I wasn't but eighteen at the time but I was right big and manly for my age and when he made a grab for me I had to hit him and when he lit I had to stomp him a little to keep him quiet until I got away. I knew Mr. Phelps wouldn't be in a reasoning mood because I could still hear him quacking and hollering inside the lodge and he just never would believe that I had been at the window just to help him.

So I ran down to my boat and headed home. I had it all figured out. Gumbo was killing them ducks and catching them fish and Mr. Phelps wasn't doing anything but having fun with girls. But I never said a word about it or even hinted at it until about nine years later when I was applying for the job of Chief of Police of Greenhill.

Mr. Phelps was Mayor then, too, and Kip Belton, thanks to the Belton fortune, was Police Commissioner. They were interviewing the applicants and Kip was making it just as difficult for me as he could. He had always resented me and, as he had married Lacey just a few months before, he resented me more than ever.

So he said that he just couldn't understand me wanting a policeman's job that didn't pay but thirty-six hundred dollars a year, when I could make twenty thousand dollars a year playing professional football. "Just how do you explain this, Peters?" He smirked in his superior way. "Not even *you* are that dumb."

Well, the main reason I wanted to be Chief of Police was to bring law and order and justice back to Greenhill by delivering Lacey and the rest of the people from him and his kind. He was always posing as a wealthy, civic-minded young leader of society, but everybody knew that on the sly he was a drunken degenerate and did such low and cruel things, especially to girls, that he wasn't fit to live.

And being only human I wanted to kill him myself because of the circumstances of his and Lacey's marriage but naturally I was too much of a Christian just to up and kill him. However, if I was a Chief of Police, sworn to enforce the law, and he should place himself above the law as was his wont in his drunken fits, then he would be a menace to society and I would be violating my sacred oath of office if I *didn't* kill him.

But to have told him that would have been to slow the Lord's work so I just gave him some of my other reasons for wanting to be Chief. I told him that as far as the football job went, money never had made much difference to me and besides that I wanted to be near my mother and since the people of Greenhill had always been so nice to me I would like to serve them if I could.

He just laughed at that and said I was even stupider than he thought and he would really have to turn me down. Besides, he said, I never had had any police experience and wouldn't know how to handle all the drunks and thugs, etc., that I would run up against.

Well, I had to give him some reference so I told him that I had had a little experience in that line—I had handled Gumbo Smith at a lodge up the river once when I was only eighteen and Gumbo was tougher than any thug in Greenhill.

Now that was all I told him about the incident and it didn't make any impression on him at all, because I don't think he'd ever seen Gumbo, but it sure made an impression on Mr. Phelps. His head looked like a barber pole it turned so many colors. Then he had a coughing fit but finally he pulled himself together and said, well, in view of my war record in Korea and being a deacon, etc., I might just make out real well as a chief of police and the job was mine.

Kip wanted to argue about it but then he must have got to thinking how, as Police Commissioner, he could order me around so he finally said it was all right with him and then he left.

With that, Mr. Phelps got up and closed the door and then stood there staring at me like he didn't know whether to kill me or kiss me. Then he got a big nasty smile on his face and came over and stuck his hand out and said he wanted to congratulate me.

He said anybody who could see what I saw at that lodge and sit on it for nine years, had the patience, the will power, the brains and all the other virtues that went in to making a real, first-class, blue ribbon sonofabitch.

"And, if there is anything I admire," he said, "it's a first-class, blue ribbon sonofabitch. A man who can keep his mouth shut, a man who can bide his time, a man who can put a noose around your neck and act like it's a bow tie."

Well, I tried explaining to him that I *hadn't* put any noose around his neck, that I had just been using the incident as a reference not as any threat, that I never had and never would say anything more about it than I had, but he just smiled wider and started asking me what I was up to, what I *really* wanted to be Chief of Police for.

I told him I wasn't up to anything but serving the people of Greenhill but if he didn't believe me I wasn't going to take the job, I would resign right then. He wouldn't hear of that, though. He started apologizing and saying we were friends and then he started explaining his situation. He said he did his drinking, etc., on the sly just so that he could keep getting elected mayor and keep running the town. If he didn't, another crowd would take over and triple the taxes on his mill and his real estate and bleed him white. But as long as he kept acting godly publicly he was going to have the godly vote and that would keep him in the driver's seat.

"And as long as I'm in the driver's seat," he said, "I'll play right along with you—even if you won't tell me what we're playing."

And despite me continually trying to explain the goodness of my intentions, that was the way things had gone. Not outwardly. On the surface, he was always sighing and telling people I was a nice boy but a stupid boy but then he would turn right around and laugh at those people behind their backs for being stupid enough to think that I was stupid.

But the worst thing was me being the only confiding friend he had. He never talked to anybody else about women or drinking, just about business and church work, so he would store up all his ugly thoughts about sex, etc., and as soon as he would get me by myself he would let fly. And that was how I had come to dread Sundays.

And this morning he kept right on talking about Pert and Lacey until he saw Sam Bates, the druggist, and Phil Gaunt, the grocer, going down the aisle from the other vestibule. You could tell they had hangovers because they were walking like they had broken glass in their shoes.

Mr. Phelps watched them going down the aisle and said, "Hah, if they think they got pains now just wait until their wives find out they were at Rita Singleton's last night."

Usually I didn't pay any attention to his ugly tales but when he mentioned Rita Singleton I figured it was in line of duty for me to inquire further, so I asked him if he knew what had happened out there.

"Thank the dear Lord I don't know," he said. "I wouldn't go within a hundred miles of that woman. All I hear is that they went out there and that's all their wives need to hear."

That was the truth. Rita Singleton was old Turk Singleton's young widow. Turk had been a rich bachelor and had spent seventy years tomcatting and drinking and defying all the women in town to marry him off. The best they could do was prophesy a miserable end for him. They kept telling their husbands, who envied Turk, that his juices would dry up and his loins would wither and he would die a bitter, lonesome, old man longing for the loving hand of a kindly wife.

Well, when Turk got to be seventy, he got a touch of the palsy and the high-blood and Doc Hackett told him that he had better cut out all his tomcatting and drinking, and all the women in town started telling their husbands, "I told you so!" But Turk said he wasn't afraid of dying and, if he had to die, he wasn't going to die in any rocking chair, he was going to die in action.

So Turk left town for about a month and all the sour, elderly ladies were hoping he had sneaked off to a sanitarium but instead he came back married to Rita. She was about twenty-three and one of the prettiest, evilest looking girls you ever saw. She had soft, black hair down to her shoulders and big, lashy brown eyes and a figure that made Charlie Few run into the Confederate monument the first time he saw her. He claimed he got a bug in his eye but all the men said they knew what he had got in his eye.

Turk didn't make any bones about it. He told everybody that he had scouted all over the south looking for the prettiest bed partner he could find and he had found Rita working in an orange juice stand down around Tarpon Springs. He had put it to her straight, he said. He told her that he was a doomed seventy-year-old bachelor worth a half million dollars and wanted a beautiful love-starved young wife to leave that half million to. How soon she collected it would just depend on her.

Well, when the women of Greenhill heard about that, most of them said it was just too vile to be allowed and Miss Della Starnes and a couple of elderly maiden ladies wanted me to run Rita out of town. They had all courted Turk at one time or the other and they had all been looking forward to him spending his last days under the care of his eighty-five-year-old Aunt Mary, who was a temperance worker and knew the Book of Revelations by heart.

But Turk just laughed at them and built Rita a real pretty place out on River Road and then spent the next six months drinking and funning about dying in action. All the men in town but me and a few others thought he was a real sport, but then one morning the news got out that he was under an oxygen tent down at the Clinic and had Reverend Samuels on one side of him and his Aunt Mary on the other side and Rupe Hobson, the lawyer, under the tent with him, changing his will.

His Aunt Mary put out the report that the Lord had appeared to him in a dream and the shock had been too much for him, but everything was all right now because he had made his peace and was just waiting to be gathered unto his fathers, glory be.

The way Doc Hackett told it, though, it wasn't exactly like that. He said that Turk and Rita had been having fun and Turk got to having so much fun that he had a heart attack. And when the pain hit him, he must have seen the Devil, in person, crooking his finger at him because he told Rita to get out of the house, and then he crawled over to the phone and called Doc and gasped for him to bring the Reverend and Aunt Mary and any other praying Christians he could pick up along the way.

He lasted two days under the tent and left off praying long enough to will half his money to Aunt Mary and the other half to the church and the W.C.T.U. Rupe Hobson, the lawyer, kept telling him he had better leave Rita a little something but every time he mentioned that name Turk would have another attack.

His funeral was a mighty big occasion for the Christian element and Miss Della and her friends nearly warped the pews with their tears, and would've done worse if Rita hadn't been there. She wore the tightest black dress I ever saw at a burying and the weepers would have to knock off every now and then to mumble something nasty about her.

But Turk wasn't able to cut her out of his money. She claimed a widow's share or something and brought a document to court that she and Turk had drawn up about their arrangement. It contained all the lurid details and when Rita let Aunt Mary see it in private, Aunt Mary came out shrieking that she would rather give Rita all the money than let that filthy thing go into any court. She later claimed it was a forgery but it was too late then. She got a third, the church got a third and Rita settled for a third.

But what distressed the women most was that Rita didn't sell her house and leave. She said that she just loved Greenhill because it had the nicest, friendliest men, especially the married ones, and she was going to spend the rest of her days out in her little love-nest by the river being a friend to man.

Well, there wasn't a day after that that somebody's wife didn't call me up at the Station wanting to know when I was going to do my duty and run Rita out of town. Sam Bates's wife kept complaining that she couldn't go into Sam's drugstore without seeing that gaudy tramp draped over the soda fountain and Sam, himself, behind it making her a malt or something. Sam claimed the only reason he did it was that he wasn't affected by her charms like his soda jerks were, that they were always getting their hands caught in the shake machine.

And Phil Gaunt's wife was the same way. She said a Christian woman couldn't get waited on in Phil's supermarket any more because Phil and all his clerks would be helping that Jezebel pick out a cut of meat or they would be candling eggs for her or pinching tomatoes to see that she got the best ones.

But there wasn't anything I could do because Rita wasn't selling her favors or even giving 'em away. She was paying the wives of the town back for the way they had treated her. What she liked to do was to lure out the husband of some woman who had snooted her and get him all smeared up with her lipstick and reeking of her perfume and then send him home. Like she did Chad Means. He's real bald-headed and Rita got him awfully drunk and took her lipstick and wrote his wife a note on top of his head. Chad didn't even know it was there until he leaned over to kiss his wife. She erased it with a big lamp they had.

As for bachelors they didn't have much better luck, if you could call it luck, either. I was one of the few that she was ever real chummy with and that was because I felt kind of sorry for her. Way down deep I think she had hoped to come to Greenhill and be respectable, but when Turk got through spreading his tales about their arrangement she never had a chance.

So I always tried to help her when I could and when she would call about some drunk trying to force his way into her house I would always go out personally and tend to it. Now I'll admit she did want to have relations with me but I think that was just because she realized I didn't want to have relations with her. Or, at least, that I *wouldn't* have relations with her whether I wanted to or not. The Lord will forgive a man getting into one woman's trap but if his life is going to be just one long trapline there ain't any forgiveness.

At any rate Rita wasn't the painted woman that wives thought she was and she wasn't the sex maniac that husbands liked to think she was, but she was a trouble-maker and that's why I was trying to get some information out of Mr. Phelps about what had gone on out there. I knew if word got out that there had been a party at her place, half the women in town would be calling to know if their husbands had been on the guest list.

But, as usual, Mr. Phelps wasn't any help. He said he didn't know what had happened and then he started talking nasty about me having relations with Rita. Being suspicious like he was, he kept saying that I wasn't running out there all the time just to shoo drunks off.

So I just ignored him after that and concentrated on my ushering. Then, when the preaching started, I went in and sat down in the back pew where the ushers always sit, but I sat as far toward the middle as I could, trying to stay away from Mr. Phelps, but I couldn't.

He sat right in my lap practically and started looking at Reverend Samuels and nodding his head and then turning and whispering to me like he was agreeing with some point that the Reverend had just made. The Reverend just loved that and it would have broke his heart to know that Mr. Phelps was really debating who he would rather go to bed with, Pert or Lacey.

I ignored him steady, though, and finally he started talking about the way the Reverend was making Sam and Phil and all the rest of the whisky drinkers in the congregation jump. And they were really jumping because every time the Reverend found out there had been a Stag Night out at the Country Club the night before, he would make his services just as noisy as he could.

He would pick out songs with high, reedy notes and then he would pray until every whisky drinker with a bowed head would think that it was going to fall off in his lap and then he would start preaching and bellow and bang on the altar so loud that whisky drinkers would almost weep, they would want to escape so bad.

But then Mr. Phelps stopped chuckling and started going "psst" at me. I finally had to turn and see what he wanted and he pointed toward the side door at the front of the church and there was my Assistant Chief of Police Delbert Tate.

He was standing some back from the door motioning for somebody to punch Dr. Winston. Now that wasn't alarming because every Sunday almost we would have to come down and call a doctor or a vet out, but the sight of Delbert in a church, or around mixed company any place, always made me a little uneasy.

He was a tall, tow-headed, rawhide boy about my age and we had been classmates in Greenhill High but when I went to college to play football he had started running whisky and causing Dawd Rankin, the Sheriff, all sorts of trouble.

It wasn't the whisky Dawd objected to so much as it was Delbert's driving. He said bootleggers had been running whisky through the county at eighty-five miles an hour or so for years but that wasn't good enough for Delbert, he had to be a smart aleck. He was hitting one hundred thirty miles an hour at times and a man just didn't dare go out on the roads at night unless he knew where Delbert was, and that it would just have to stop.

Then war came along and I was Delbert's sergeant in the Marines over in Korea and did him a few services and he got right attached to me. Then, when we came home and I was named Chief of Police, Dawd asked me if I wouldn't please put Delbert on the Force so he wouldn't start terrorizing the county again. So I took Delbert on and although he had broke the spirit of every hot-rodder and bootlegger we had, he still wasn't what you would call a polished police officer, especially in his talk.

So that's why I was a little uneasy about him, especially when I saw that he looked right wrought up. But finally somebody punched Dr. Winston and he go up and eased out to where

Delbert was. I saw them talk a few seconds and then leave and I settled back and didn't think any more about it.

But then, about a minute later, I heard somebody come in the vestibule right behind us. Mr. Phelps and I both turned around and there Delbert was sticking his head in the door. I didn't know what to make of it because he was real red in the face and tears were all puddled up in his eyes and he was trying to say something but couldn't. Finally he just stuck his head in the door a little further and just blurted it out.

"Buck, some bastard's murdered Rita!"

CHAPTER TWO

WELL, when Delbert blurted that out, I guess it was like when people heard that somebody had murdered Lincoln. I jumped about as high as them whisky drinkers had been jumping and Mr. Phelps, who had heard him too, he jumped and said, *"Good God!"* He didn't mean to say it as loud as he did and Charlie Few, sitting about three pews down with his wife, heard him and turned around and glared like he had never heard such language before.

Then, before I could stop him, Mr. Phelps had leaned forward and whispered to Charlie what had happened. The blood drained out of Charlie's face and he forgot where he was and said a dirty word that shook people up for about five pews down, and before I could hustle Delbert outside the news was spreading fast and most of the men looked like they thought Charlie had been putting it real mildly.

Delbert and I didn't waste any time talking once we got outside because I knew Mr. Phelps would probably try following us as soon as he finished gloating over the looks on everybody's faces. So we just hopped in Delbert's squad car and headed on out Main Street toward River Road.

I didn't say anything for a while though because Delbert still had tears in his eyes and was all choked up. He had been trying to court Rita, I knew, but I had no idea he felt so tender about her and I was real touched. But finally he gave the steering wheel a whack and snarled, "Shot right out from under me, by God! One more week and I would have had that for sure!"

Well, that was right disillusioning but at least it dissolved the lump in his throat enough for him to talk and he started telling me about it. He said that Mattie Mason, Rita's cook, had called him at the station around 10:30 and had been crying and bawling so that he couldn't make out anything she said except that something had happened to Miss Rita.

So he had high-tailed it out to Rita's and sure enough something had happened to her. Somebody had sneaked up to her bedroom window during the night and shot through the screen and sprayed the room and all its contents with a .38. Mattie had come to work around ten o'clock like she usually did on Sunday mornings and there Rita was sprawled out on the bed with a bullet in her head. It had happened at 3:37 evidently because one of the bullets had ricocheted into the electric clock beside the bed and stopped it at that time.

"I just don't know what to think of a man with a brain that twisted," Delbert almost sobbed. "With all the ugly women in town he could have killed, the sonofabitch had to shoot her."

Like I've said Greenhill is on a big sloping hill in a bend of the river. The town is on top of the hill and so are most of the homes but the people with money have got their homes either on the brow of the hill or the slope on either side of River Road.

Rita's house was on the river side of the road and, to get to it, you had to go down this side road leading to an old abandoned dock on the river. About halfway down the road was Rita's driveway. It wound through some oaks and beeches for about fifty yards and there was the love-nest as old Turk had called it. It was a real pretty ranch-type brick house with picture windows and a brick terrace around the front so you could sit out on it and look at the river about a half mile down the slope.

Dr. Winston—he was the doctor and the coroner Delbert had called out of church—had his car parked in the side yard when we got there and poor old Mattie was sitting out back in the patio dabbing at her eyes with a handkerchief. As soon as we drove up she started sobbing and came out to the car and said I had to do something.

"Mr. Buck," she said, "Dr. Winston's done called the undertaker to come get Miss Rita and he told him that it wasn't any murder, that she committed suicide!"

Well, with that Delbert's mouth fell open and then he said, "Suicide! Has he lost his damn mind?" and then he started to rush into the house after him, but I grabbed him and told him that I would handle Dr. Winston.

"No, by God," he said, "you'll let him treat you like an idiot child like you always do and I'm sick and tired of that bastard's airy ways and I don't care how many letters he's got behind his name he ain't telling me that girl shot herself."

Now he had a point about Dr. Winston's ways. He was a big, tall, paunchy, black-haired fellow about forty-five and although he had too much nose and no more chin than a chicken he thought he was a real dog with the ladies and was real arrogant although he hadn't always been that way. When he had come to Greenhill about twenty years before he would treat anything that walked, talked or crawled just so long as it had fifty cents in its pocket.

But when he had fooled enough people with his oily, fawning ways and built himself up a good practice he turned into a society doctor and for a poor man to get him out of bed at night on a call he would have to set his mattress on fire. And, like some other members of his social set, he thought our police department was just for arresting mill-hands and Negroes and that all we were supposed to do to him and his set was drive them home when we found them drunk.

So he never had been much help to us as a coroner but I had my reasons for letting him treat me like an idiot, although Delbert didn't know it. "Buck," he whined trying to get loose from me, "you *know* what he's trying to do. If he can cover this thing up as a suicide and stop us from investigating it, the husbands in this town will raise a statue to him."

Well, I knew that was what he was trying to do but I knew that he wasn't going to succeed so I told Mattie to run on home for a while and I'd talk to her later and then I said, "Delbert, if you will just relax and keep quiet I will tell you why Dr. Winston ain't going to call this a suicide and if he does the only statue to be raised to him will be a tombstone."

He looked real baffled at that and asked me if I meant I had something on Dr. Winston. I gave him a little lecture. "Delbert," I said, "I've made you be respectful to Dr. Winston and Kip Belton and people like that and you've hated it. I told you that the way of such transgressors was not so smooth and that the Lord would deliver them into our hands but you wouldn't believe me. Well, delivery has just been made on Dr. Winston and, if you will promise to keep quiet until the right time, I will tell you what I know about him."

He promised and, when I told him what I knew about Dr. Winston, he did keep quiet. In fact, I never saw him so quiet. He stared at me and then he said, "I'll be a sonofabitch," and then he got real respectful, like I was J. Edgar Hoover or somebody, and ushered me through the kitchen door. Then we went out into the hall and down to Rita's room. It wasn't so big but it was sure fancy—silk drapes, two-tone wallpaper, a carpet that you mired up in and a big mirror on the ceiling over the bed.

When we first walked in, though, there wasn't any sign of Dr. Winston but then he backed out of Rita's big walk-in closet with a sheepish look on his face. I knew what he had been hunting in the closet but all I said was good morning. He just grunted like we weren't worth speaking to and then he sat down on the stool to Rita's fancy dressing table and started writing in a pad.

While he was acting so official, Delbert and I looked around the room and it was just like Delbert had said. There were four bullet holes in the window screen. Two of the bullets had hit over the head board of the bed, another one had hit the wall and ricocheted into the clock and the fourth one was in Rita.

She was on the big, wide bed that Turk had had custom built and, while I didn't want to do it, I forced myself to pull back the bloody sheet a little and look at her. The bullet had hit her between the right cheekbone and the ear and the sight of what it had done to her head made me want to vomit, but it didn't make me so sick that I couldn't see there weren't any powder burns.

"If that girl wasn't killed," Delbert whispered, "then Custer wasn't either!"

Well, Dr. Winston must have overheard him because he started to say something but just then he saw Mr. Phelps drive up outside so he snapped his pad shut and went out to greet him. Delbert got worried all over again because he was afraid that Mr. Phelps might side with Dr. Winston on the verdict and, if we didn't agree with it, he would have Kip Belton fire us.

"And you know what that Belton will do then," he said. "He'll make Chastain Chief of Police and he'll agree to anything."

I told him to stop worrying because Mr. Phelps hated Dr. Winston too, although Dr. Winston didn't know it. He had treated Mr. Phelps's wife for a nervous rash and had told her that she ought to have a hobby such as going fishing with Mr. Phelps. Well, she did and she was crazy about it and Mr. Phelps wound up with the nervous rash. A lot of times he would have a girl waiting for him up at the lodge but his wife would see him heading for his boat and say that she wanted to go fishing too and instead of spending the afternoon with the girl he would spend it picking backlashes out of his wife's line. I thought it was pretty funny but Mr. Phelps didn't and he had just been waiting for a chance to get even with Dr. Winston.

But when we heard him and Dr. Winston coming down Rita's hallway, you would have thought they were the best of friends. Dr. Winston was explaining the details of the case and Mr. Phelps was gushing about how thankful he was that Greenhill had such a competent coroner.

That got Delbert worried again but I told him that the friendlier Mr. Phelps got the more you had to watch out for him. "And I ain't ever heard him this friendly before!" I said.

And I hadn't. He strolled into the room with his arm around Dr. Winston's shoulder like he had adopted him or something.

"Well, Buck," he beamed, "I hear we got all excited for nothing. Dr. Winston tells me it wasn't murder after all, just plain old suicide."

I could tell that he knew Dr. Winston was lying but Dr. Winston didn't suspect a thing. "Certainly, it was suicide," he said, like he dared me to say anything back and then he went into the details. First he explained the motive he had dreamed up. He said that Rita had been telling everybody that she had been going to that doctor in Memphis about some sort of back trouble, but he had had confidential talk with that doctor and found out it wasn't her back, it was cancer.

And then, he went on, Rita with her twisted mind had probably figured that everybody would gloat over her misfortune and her suicide so she had decided to make it look like she had been killed and that would call for an investigation and she could cause as many innocent people trouble leaving this life as she had living it.

"So," he said, "she fired four shots into the room from outside that window, came back into the room, and knowing that Dick Tracy and his friend here would call it murder, she put the fifth bullet in that diseased brain of hers."

Mr. Phelps pursed his lips and shook his head like he was agreeing to everything so Dr. Winston kept right on going. He reached into his coat pocket and pulled out a pistol wrapped in a handkerchief and said that it was the gun Rita used and since there were powder burns on her face that's all there was to it. "Suicide, Phelps, pure and simple."

Mr. Phelps nodded and said it sure looked like suicide, but then he turned to me and drawled, "What do you think, Buck?"

Just like he had figured on, Dr. Winston acted all hurt and surprised and wanted to know what difference it made what I thought, *he* was the coroner. Mr. Phelps acted real apologetic about that and said that it didn't really make any difference. "I know he's not the criminologist that you, Winston, are but he is the Chief of Police and we should do him the courtesy of asking his opinion, don't you think?"

Now that made Dr. Winston feel a lot better. He thought that Mr. Phelps was just being real coy and making fun of my stupidity, so he gave me a pitying little smirk and said, "All right, Buck, what *do* you think?"

Well, it was like a mouse smarting off to a cat but I couldn't help feeling kind of sorry for him so I let him off as easy as I could. I told him that I thought he was joking about it being suicide but now that he'd had his little joke I thought he ought to put Rita's pistol back in the drawer of the night table where he had gotten it from and tell Mr. Phelps that Rita really didn't have any powder burns on her and that it was murder not suicide.

He just didn't know how to take that. It was the first time I had ever stood up to him and he got real red in the face and looked like he wanted to hop on me, and then he looked like he wanted to hop on Delbert, but then he saw how Delbert was drooling for him to try it, so then he looked around for Mattie to hop on. But as she was gone he turned on Mr. Phelps.

"Phelps," he snarled, "did I hear him right?"

"Dr. Winston," I said, "Delbert has got four .38 hulls he found right outside that window and Mattie will swear to it. They couldn't have been fired from that pistol of Rita's you got in your pocket because it's a .32."

With that he knew I had him trapped but he wasn't really worried because he thought his dear friend, Mr. Phelps, was going to pull him out of it. So he gave this wild, sneering laugh and said, "He *is* an idiot, Phelps. You told me he was stupid but

27

you didn't tell me he was *this* stupid. Buck, don't you *know* what we're doing?"

Well, that was his death rattle because Mr. Phelps blinked at him like some innocent, bewildered old man and said, "Wait a minute, Winston. What *are* we doing?"

Dr. Winston stared at him like he couldn't believe it. Then he gave a nervous little laugh and said, "I'm calling this suicide. *I'm* the coroner. Don't you get it?"

Mr. Phelps just blinked at him again and said, "Get what? You mean it's *not* a suicide? You mean Buck is right, it's a murder?"

Dr. Winston shook his head like he was talking to a fool and right then I realized just how vain and arrogant a man he was. Instead of suspicioning that Mr. Phelps was baiting him, he just thought how dumb Mr. Phelps was and how he had over-estimated his smartness just because he was a millionaire.

"My God, Phelps," he wheezed, "don't you realize that we've *got* to call this a suicide? If we call it a murder, the investigation will blow this town wide open. There'll be broken homes, wives chasing husbands through the streets, children orphaned ... damn it, man, you're the Mayor. Think of your community. I'm thinking of it. I'm trying to save my friends, your friends ..."

It was a mighty touching oration but I thought it had gone on long enough, so I stopped him and told him that he wasn't thinking about his friends, that all he was thinking about was saving himself.

"Dr. Winston," I said, "I know all about you and Rita Singleton and I know that you swore to kill her."

Well, for about ten seconds nobody said a word. Delbert knew what was coming so he just winked at Dr. Winston like he was a mighty naughty boy. Mr. Phelps didn't know what was coming but he was drooling anyway because he sensed that I really knew something or I never would have made a charge like I did. As for Dr. Winston, his blood started running so cold that his glasses were almost frosting up.

"*You* are insinuating that *I* did this?" he snarled.

"I ain't insinuating anything," I said. "I'm telling you that you had every reason for wanting to kill her and if you don't stop trying to cover this thing up I'm going to charge you with doing it."

"Charge *me* with murdering her?" he said. "I'm the one man that never went near that slut."

Mr. Phelps saw how he was sweating and he knew he was lying so he went into his dumb act again. "Now you look here, Buck," he said real sternly, "I know Holland Winston. He might cover up for his friends because he's true blue but..."

Dr. Winston sighed and cut him off and said he appreciated his help but would he please just let him handle things. He was stalling for time, trying to figure out if I really knew something, and Mr. Phelps knew what he was doing so he kept right on him.

"No, sir, Winston," he said, "*I'll* handle this. You're a friend of mine and I won't have you slandered this way. Why would you want to murder Rita? You never went near her. You're a devoted family man. You've got a lovely wife, two lovely children and..."

That was more than Dr. Winston could stand so he said, "Damn it, Phelps, will you please shut up?" and with that Mr. Phelps knew he had hit a nerve so he looked real hurt and real concerned.

"Winston, my boy," he said real fatherly, "you *didn't* go near her?"

Dr. Winston ignored him and stared at me and then he stared at Rita's body and I knew just what he was thinking. She was dead so it would be just my word against his. "Of course, I didn't go near her!" he snapped at Mr. Phelps. "I never even talked to the bitch."

With that I sighed and told him that I had tried to be as easy on him as I could, but he wouldn't let me so I was going to have to tell him a story that Rita had told me. "And," I said, "I'm going to try and tell it just the way she did so that you will recognize the truthfulness of the details. Now sit down!"

So he sat down but it was more like he was crouching to spring than sitting and then he said, "Peters, you're going to tell a damn lie about me right in front of the Mayor of this town and when you do I'm going to sue you for every penny, every..."

"*Sue* him!" Mr. Phelps snorted. "We'll jail him. Now out with it, Peters. What did Rita ever do to this fine Christian that would make him want to kill her? Out with it, sir!"

He was so anxious to hear it that he was almost as nervous as Dr. Winston. "Dr. Winston," I said, "I'm sorry I've got to tell this because it's the story of how you trailed Rita into Memphis one day and tried to buy her body and what happened to you as a result."

Well, the way the blood drained out of his face you would have thought his feet were leaking and Mr. Phelps didn't help things a bit. He let out this big gasp and said, "Dr. Holland Winston *buying a girl's body?* You know you're lying, Peters!"

"Phelps," Dr. Winston wheezed, trying to act bored instead of panic-struck, "we both know he's lying, so will you just let him go ahead and get it out of his system? I appreciate your support but will you *please* be quiet?"

"All right, Winston," Mr. Phelps said real subdued like, "but I just don't see how you can sit there so calm and collected while..."

"*Get on with your damn story!*" Dr. Winston screeched

"Well, Dr. Winston," I said, "this is the story as Rita told it to me: One day about three months ago you trailed her into Memphis and she knew you did because she kept catching glimpses of your car in her rear-view mirror. Then, when you got to Memphis, you accidentally on purpose bumped into her on the street and acted real surprised and asked her to have a drink.

"Then you took her into one of those dimly lit bars and sat in the very last booth way in back and after a couple of drinks you started warming up to her. You said you had been wanting to get her alone ever since she had come to Greenhill and then you started playing with her legs. Then when you got your hand as far up as her knees you announced that you weren't like the rest of these juvenile delinquents in Greenhill, you were an adult and not only a doctor but a businessman so you would get right to the point. You would give her a hundred dollars to spend the night with you.

"Well, you didn't realize it but you made Rita mighty mad with that. She was a wild girl but she wasn't any whore. Turk had bought her favors in a way but he had had to marry her to close the deal so she decided that she would teach you a lesson that you never would forget.

"So, instead of slapping you at the mention of money, she just smiled and let you slip your hand up a little farther, and then she started playing with your legs and said that she didn't believe in one-night stands but that for five thousand dollars you could have her for a year any time you could slip off and see her."

Mr. Phelps couldn't stand it any longer. "Peters," he gasped, "are you trying to tell me that Dr. Holland Winston, Greenhill's leading physician, was sitting in a public place letting a girl play with his legs, letting her fondle him?"

Naturally that got Dr. Winston all upset again. "You old sonofabitch," he bellowed, "if you don't shut up I'm going to fondle you!" And naturally that got Mr. Phelps upset and he acted real hurt again and said real prissy, "*Well,* Winston, I was merely trying to defend you. If somebody told *you* that a girl was playing with *my* legs..."

"Damn it, she wasn't playing with my legs!"

"Well, what *was* she playing with?"

Dr. Winston almost started weeping at that and told Mr. Phelps that he had told him ten times I was lying and would he please, please quit trying to help him. So Mr. Phelps sighed and said all right and I started in again.

"Well, Dr. Winston," I said, "when Rita told you that her body would cost you five thousand dollars you whimpered that she must be out of her mind, but she wasn't because she gave you a little squeeze and you quivered and staggered to your feet and told her to wait right there. Then you went down the street to a bank where you must have a safety deposit box full of untaxed money and then, not knowing that Rita had followed you, you came back to the booth with fifty one-hundred-dollar bills.

"Rita counted them out while you played with her legs some more and then you all got in your car and went out to the Marybelle Tourist Cabins where Rita knew Tom French, the proprietor. Then you all went down to a cabin and you started pawing Rita, but she stopped you and said that she ought to call Greenhill and break the date she had for that night.

"You said to hell with her date but she said that it was with a very good friend of hers and that, if she didn't give him some excuse, she would have to leave in a couple of hours but other-wise she would love to spend the night with you. The thought of that just drove you mad and you said fine. So she told you to get all undressed and showered and ready for her and then she left and you thought she was headed for the phone but she wasn't.

"Instead she went around the cabin, watched you through the window, and when you got in the shower she came back in the cabin and said she had forgot her change purse. But instead of getting her change purse, she got your car keys, your shoes, your socks, every stitch of clothes you had, and left.

"Then she got in your car and went back into Memphis and picked up her car and came on back home. And during all that time and more you were trapped stark naked in that cabin with your lovely wife thinking you were at a medical meeting in Little Rock.

"But right after dark, Tom French, the proprietor, who knew what Rita had done, heard this rapping on the back window of his office and he looked out and thought the Ku Klux or an Arab was after him but it was just you wrapped in a sheet. He told Rita later that you had it wrapped around your face too and the only thing sticking out was those black horn-rimmed spectacles and that you were the damnedest looking sight he ever saw, especially when his poodle started barking and snapping at you because it hadn't ever seen anything like you either.

"But he let you in and you told him some fantastic lie about how Rita was your wife and the worst sort of practical joker and had run off with your car and clothes. He played it innocent and dressed you in some clothes of his that were so short in the arms and legs that you looked even more ridiculous than you did in the sheet. Then he took you into Memphis and there was your car in the parking lot where Rita had left it.

"You must have sneaked in home around four o'clock in the morning and what you told your wife nobody knows, but it must have been even more fantastic than what you told Tom French. Then the next day you bumped into Rita in Sam Bates's drugstore. She was real bright and cheery and asked you how you liked her new Cadillac convertible she had just bought.

"You knew she had bought it with your money so you told her out loud that you thought it was real pretty, but you told her under your breath that if she didn't give you your money and your clothes back you were going to kill her. She just laughed and walked out and she never gave your money back nor your clothes because that's what you were hunting for in the closet when Delbert and I first walked in here."

Now that was the story and Dr. Winston knew it was the truth because his face was so ashy you could've shook clinkers out of his ears and Mr. Phelps knew it was the truth by just look-ing at him and the only thing that kept him from rolling on the floor and howling was that he wanted to torture Dr. Winston some more.

"By George, Peters," the Mayor raged at me, "I'm not ordi-narily a cursing man but I must say that is the damnedest, the most disgusting, the most sordid lie I ever heard. Make him prove it, Winston. Make him show you just one shred of proof."

"Phelps," Dr. Winston sighed, trying to rally his dignity, "*I* know it's a lie, *you* know it's a lie. That's all I care about. I am not going to dignify the thing by asking for proof!"

"Oh, yes, you are!" Mr. Phelps said. "Like you say, I am the Mayor of this community and it's my duty to look out after my people and I won't have a police officer of mine engaging in such vile, such filthy, such... Where's your proof, Peters? Right now! Where is it?"

I knew it was going to look bad me knowing so much about Rita's bedroom and about Rita personally, too, but it couldn't be helped. So I went over to her dressing table and got a key out of her jewelry box and went into the closet and opened up a trunk. In it was Dr. Winston's suit. It was a real expensive, light blue, woman-chasing model, and anybody in town would have recognized it as his even if it hadn't had his initials on the inside pocket. I brought it out and held it up for them to see.

"Why, Winston!" Mr. Phelps said, like he was almost going to weep. "It *wasn't* a lie. She really was fondling you. That *is* your suit!"

That's when Delbert got back into things. "Suit!" he leered. "It may be his suit now but if he don't start talking it's gonna be his shroud."

Dr. Winston didn't know what to do so he just did what came natural to him. He started acting arrogant again. "Well, damn it, Phelps," he snarled, "don't just stand there! Fire the bastards! Call Kip Belton. He'll fire 'em."

Delbert let out a cackle. "You just do that, Mr. Phelps! You go ahead and fire us because we got our social security right here!" And with that he gave Dr. Winston a playful little poke in the ribs and said, "What's your wife's phone number?"

Dr. Winston didn't look mad any more, he looked like he was going to cry and I almost felt sorry for him again. I told him that I thought that Delbert was kidding about blackmailing him but even if he wasn't kidding I wouldn't let him. And I wouldn't. Blackmailing a man for money is a sin. But if you blackmail him to improve his soul, that's missionary work. Delbert wasn't any missionary though.

"You can't stop me, Buck," he said. "All I got to do is walk in Steve Hagerman's poolroom, tell the boys about this sonofabitch creeping around in that sheet with a poodle snapping at his butt and I'll have him laughed out of town by sundown."

Dr. Winston knew it was the truth because everybody in town that he had snooted and treated like dirt was laying for him. Mr. Phelps knew it too and he acted broken-hearted.

"Winston," he sighed, "I'll still fire 'em, if you say so, but I'm afraid he's got you. You could swear this suit was stolen and planted here but that motel owner has got a sample of your handwriting on his register and he could probably get the bartender at that place where Rita was fondling you to ..."

"All right, Phelps," he almost sobbed, "all right, I hear you, damn it, I hear you!" Then he turned and whined that I knew he hadn't killed Rita and I said I sure hoped he hadn't but he did have the motive and he'd been trying mighty hard to pass it off as a suicide. He admitted that and apologized for everything past and present and said he could prove that, at the time of the murder, he had been at the Clinic delivering a baby. Then he almost got down on his knees. "Now, can I please have that suit, Buck?"

Delbert just laughed and told him that he must be out of his mind, that the suit was impounded until the case was solved. "And then you'll have to give us a sworn statement that the suit found in Rita Singleton's trunk was yours and explain how it got there."

"But don't worry about it, Dr. Winston," I said, "won't a thing be said about it as long as you co-operate with the police."

"And not just in this case," Delbert said, "in all of 'em. When we call you to come look at a body, you come running. Don't go finishing no bridge game, don't go finishing no round of golf. You put that rosy, rich, medicated butt of yours in that car and you come right then, you hear me? Right then!"

Well, Dr. Winston looked so downcast that I thought I would cheer him up a little, so I told him that he wouldn't have to worry about rendering any more verdicts about the cause of death though. "Delbert and I will decide whether something is suicide or murder or not, all you will have to do is sign the report."

Now I meant that in the friendliest sort of way but he didn't take it like that at all. "Have you lost your mind?" he screamed at me. "Did you hear that, Phelps? These blackmailing bastards are going to take over this town. Don't you see it? They've got me. They can murder anybody in this town and I'll have to swear it's suicide. They're taking over. You'll be next and…"

"*Me?*" Mr. Phelps gasped, real offended. "I haven't been trying to buy any bodies, haven't any girls been fondling me."

"All right," Dr. Winston screeched, "all right! But mark my word, you pious old sonofabitch, they're taking over."

I tried telling him that it wasn't so but he just got madder. He said for me not to kid him, that he could see how I operated.

"You go around playing deacon and telling your victims they haven't got anything to worry about but all the time you've got that maniac at your side threatening to break up their homes, laugh them out of town, report them to the tax bureau. You sure got the people in this town fooled, you sanctimonious sonofabitch!"

Well, that hurt me, even coming from somebody like him, and I told him it just wasn't so. "If I wanted to take over this town, Dr. Winston," I said, "I could do it real easy because Rita left me her diary."

He screamed louder than ever then. "Diary? *Diary!* What diary?"

I opened the main drawer to Rita's dressing table and then opened up a hidden drawer inside and pulled her diary out. "This one!" I said.

He wasn't able to say anything and all Mr. Phelps could say was "My God!" but Delbert grabbed the diary and started shaking it at Dr. Winston. "We ain't *going* to take over this town!" he said, laughing real wild. "We just took it over. Law and order has finally returned to Greenhill and here's your statute book right here!"

"Get the diary, Phelps," Dr. Winston whimpered. "If I haven't got a right to my suit, that maniac hasn't got any right to that diary."

I snatched the diary back from Delbert and told Dr. Winston that I did have a right to it, a legal right. "There's a copy of Rita's will in that strong box in the trunk. It says that in case anything happens to her, Buck Peters gets her diary. You say she's been murdered so I get the diary."

Delbert reached for it and said, "What day was that you were in Memphis, Doc?" but I pushed his hand away and told him that we weren't opening the dirty thing unless it was absolutely necessary to solving the case. He told me not to start acting stupid again. "Can't I even see what she said about me?"

"No, sir," I said. "If we don't need it to help us solve the case, I'm going to burn it."

"Well, by George!" Mr. Phelps said, starting to bait Dr. Winston again, "I think that's real fair and, Winston, I think you owe him an apology."

"*Apology?*" Dr. Winston gasped. "Fair? Phelps, don't you see what the fiendish sonofabitch is doing? If he *doesn't* open the diary, *nobody* will know who's in it and he'll drive *everybody* crazy with the damn thing. Phelps, you don't run this town any more. *He* runs it. He's got every man in this town by the throat."

Well, I was getting pretty tired of his lies by then, so I told him that I had been nice enough not to book him on suspicion of murder, but that if he said one word about me taking over any town or anything about me having the diary or Mr. Phelps being a stupid old man, then the only patients he'd see would be on visitors' day.

He turned ashy and started apologizing again but when he saw me cooling off he said that he knew that I had him but could he ask me just one question. I had a good idea what was coming but I told him to go ahead. He gave a weak, nasty little smile and cut his eyes at Mr. Phelps and said, "Buck, we don't know who murdered Rita but at least we've found out who was going to bed with her and cutting everybody else in town out. It was you. Now, tell me, Deacon, how was it?"

That's the type of fellow he was. Just plain trash. The poor girl lying dead not ten feet away but he had to ask a question like that. And it wasn't just curiosity. In his own sneaky way he was letting me know that he had something on me too. But I explained it to him. I explained that I never had laid a hand on Rita but if he kept talking that way I was going to lay one on him.

"But, Buck," he said, "if you weren't going to bed with her and hadn't spent a lot of time in this room how could you know what was in her dressing table drawers and in her closet and why should she be telling you about everything?"

"Because everybody has got to have somebody they can confide in," I said, "and Rita chose me. I would come out here on a complaint and after I had run whatever drunk it was off, we would come back here, because it was Rita's favorite room, and she would tell me her troubles. She said I was the only real friend she had."

"I see," he said, cutting his eyes at Mr. Phelps again, "and all you did was talk?"

'Well," I said, "she did try to get me to have relations with her but only because she thought it would be funny having relations with a deacon and a chief of police all at the same time. But I wouldn't do it. I told her it was evil and that Christian gentlemen didn't do such things. But every time I told her that she would start taunting me and telling me how many evil Christian gentlemen there were in Greenhill."

"I see," he said, his face getting a little white and his voice getting a little strained. "And she just volunteered the information about me. You didn't ask her about me?"

"Not exactly," I said. "She kept talking about all the Christian gentlemen in Greenhill wanting to have relations with her, and I wouldn't believe her until she gave me all the names and the details, and finally I told her that I bet a fine, upstanding, happily married Christian gentleman like Dr. Holland Winston had never wanted to have relations with her and she said oh, yes, you had and then she showed me your suit and told me all about Memphis."

Well, he just stared at me for quite a few seconds and nobody said anything. Mr. Phelps whistled a little tune under his breath and studied the ceiling and Delbert whistled a little tune under his breath and studied the floor and all that sort of threw me off guard because the next thing I knew Dr. Winston had made a lunge for Delbert's pistol and was screeching, "I'll kill him, damn his soul, I'll kill him!"

Delbert was taken by surprise too and got knocked to the floor and Dr. Winston started kicking him in the side trying to get his pistol loose from his holster. Now that put me out of temper because he was a big man, well over two hundred, and a lot heavier than Delbert so I grabbed him by the throat and lifted him off the floor and started shaking him.

I shook him a little harder than I really meant to because the first thing I knew his nose started bleeding a little and a pivot tooth popped out and Mr. Phelps started beating on me saying that I was killing him. It was all for his own good, though, because when I lifted him off the floor he was a confirmed heathen and when I set him back down he was a practicing Christian. He just couldn't apologize enough. He apologized generally for his conduct of the case and then he apologized to me for his accusations and then he apologized to Delbert for kicking him and then apologized to Mr. Phelps for being such a disappointment to him.

"Well, I should hope so!" Mr. Phelps snorted. "Making a fool out of me in front of a fine officer like this. Go file your report and just remember what a pious old sonofabitch I am and what I'll do if you say one word about this fine officer trying to take over any town."

It was like warning a turpentined cat not to carry its tail so high next time. He swore that he wouldn't say a word about anything, that he was on our side, and that if we ever needed him day or night to be sure and call him. Then he slunk out of the room and headed for his car. We watched him leave, from the back door, and Delbert and Mr. Phelps just had a fit laughing. Then Mr. Phelps turned and looked at me and all of a sudden he stopped laughing. It was like he had suddenly decided he didn't have anything to laugh about.

"You really didn't go to bed with her, did you? A gorgeous woman, probably half naked, just begging and panting for you to take her, but all you did was sit there and talk about God."

"But I was on duty, Mr. Phelps," I said, "and it's a policeman's duty to keep track of the sinning going on."

"All right, you inhuman sonofabitch," he bellowed, "but you remember this! When you *do* take over this town I'm on *your* side!"

And with that he left too and then Delbert started smiling sort of funny and looking at me like he'd never really seen me before and then he started asking me what sort of hold I had over Mr. Phelps and what made him so suspicious of me. I tried explaining that Mr. Phelps was just one of those people who didn't understand Christianity in action but I was interrupted by the sound of a siren and Oscar Wright, the undertaker, that Dr. Winston had called, drove up in his ambulance.

Oscar is a little, fat, apple-cheeked fellow and pretty jolly except when he's on a call and then he looks like his mother has just been run over by a truck. But this time he didn't look sad at all. He looked mad. He charged right into the house and, instead of employing his usual doleful tones, he snarled, "Where's that sonofabitch Winston?"

Well, Delbert and I both knew something was up then because you just don't hear undertakers referring to doctors that way very often.

"Oscar," I said, "Doctor Winston's gone but he changed his mind. It wasn't suicide like he thought, it was murder."

With that he headed down the hall until he saw the bedroom and then he went in and looked at all the bullet holes in the wall and then he pulled the sheet back and looked at Rita. For a second he looked like he was almost going to cry because Rita had been a friend to him something like she had been to me but then he blinked his eyes clear and glared at us.

"I tried telling Winston over the phone that I bet this wasn't any suicide. This girl wasn't only murdered, I know who murdered her!"

Well, I stared at him and then I stared at Delbert. He didn't know what to say either because he knew as well as I did that Oscar wasn't given to talking rash. But I still couldn't believe it.

"Oscar," I said, "I hope you realize what you're about to say and I sure hope you got some positive proof before you say it."

"All I've got is a positive suspicion," he said, "but I'll bet you a funeral home and every dime I've got that I'm right."

"Who?" Delbert wheezed.

Oscar took a deep breath. "Your own Police Commissioner. That no-good bastard, Kip Belton!"

CHAPTER THREE

FOR ABOUT TEN SECONDS after Oscar said that I just stared at him. Then my blood started racing and my flesh started crawling because, if he was right, if Kip had killed Rita, then I hadn't become Chief of Police for nothing and I was finally going to get my chance to bring justice for all back to Greenhill and deliver Lacey out of his hands. So, just as gentle as if Oscar was cotton candy, I sat him down on the stool at Rita's dressing table and told him to tell me and Delbert, who was right transfixed too, all about it.

And he told us. It seemed that he had been up until one o'clock embalming Joe Fredericks, who'd been caught in a threshing machine, and he had got hungry and gone down to Sim Everette's all-night café, down by the river, to get a hot fish sandwich.

Then after he had ordered the sandwich, he had gone back to the restroom but had found it locked and two men inside arguing. It was Sam Bates and Phil Gaunt and they were both drunk. Phil was cussing and telling Sam to watch what he was doing but Sam evidently was paying him no mind because he was cussing about Phil not going back out to Rita Singleton's with him.

Well, at the mention of Rita, Oscar had kept real quiet and listened, and he gathered from the snatches of conversation he could hear that they had been out at Rita's and Kip Belton had come along and run them off. But Kip had stayed and done something to Rita that made her so mad that she'd pulled a gun on him. He had left in a drunken rage, swearing that he was going to get himself a gun and come back and shoot her.

How Sam and Phil knew about this Oscar didn't know but after Kip had left they had evidently hung around outside Rita's waiting for him to come back with the gun. After he didn't come back in an hour or so they had come down to Sim's to get something to eat. Sam wanted to go back out but Phil was arguing that Kip had gone off and passed out some place like he usually did.

"So then," Oscar said, "Sam and Phil left the café and they must not have come back out but it's a cinch that bastard Belton did. He's your man, Buck."

Naturally I was pretty disappointed in that. He had put us on Kip's trail, all right, but he sure hadn't treed him for us. Delbert, though, he was all fired up about it because he hated Kip worse than he did Dr. Winston and he grabbed the phone to call Phil Gaunt but Oscar got all horrified and stopped him. He said that we weren't supposed to say a word to nobody about what he had told us. "Just go ahead and arrest Kip Belton!"

"But, Oscar," I said, "you can't arrest a man on hearsay evidence from two drunks in a toilet."

"But, damn it," Oscar said, "I don't want Phil Gaunt knowing I told on him. He's got a dying uncle but he'll pickle the old bastard before he'll let me bury him!"

Well, I told him that his name wouldn't have to be mentioned to get Sam and Phil to talk and Delbert backed me up. He said that when they found out that we had Rita's diary they would start talking so fast it would sound like a tobacco auction.

Now that made all the difference in the world because Oscar was a bachelor and the diary didn't hold any terrors for him. He seemed real tickled about it and brightened right up and said in that case he might be burying Phil before he did his uncle. Then I helped him take poor Rita's body out to the ambulance and told him that I would contact Rita's sister in Florida about the final arrangements.

When I went back in the house, Delbert was all set to call Phil. I said not to torment him and he promised me he wouldn't but he did. Phil answered the phone like he was some big executive being disturbed and right away Delbert disguised his voice and acted like he was a stranger calling.

He first asked Phil if he was Phil Gaunt the big grocer and then, if he was Phil Gaunt, the director of the Bank of Greenhill, and then, if he was Phil Gaunt, the vice-president of the Greenhill Country Club. Well, Phil is a real pompous little fat man anyway and that recitation of his honors got him so puffed up that he thought it must be *Who's Who* or the Governor on the phone.

"Yes, I'm vice-president of the Greenhill Country Club!" he said real proud. "Who's calling?"

"The police!" said Delbert, lapsing into his own voice. "Get your fat butt out here!"

Well, it was one of the cruelest tricks I ever heard played on a man, like blowing up a paper bag just to pop it, but to have heard Phil talk you never would have known how mad it made him. All of a sudden he was the friendliest, most informal little fellow you ever heard. And the fastest thinking one, too.

"Oh," he gushed, "it's you, Reverend Samuels. I didn't recognize your voice."

Right away Delbert and I knew that his wife must be within listening range and he didn't want her thinking it was the police calling.

"Yeah," Delbert said, "this is the Reverend, all right. Reverend Delbert Tate. Me and Reverend Buck Peters are holding funeral services out at Rita Singleton's and we want you and Brother Sam Bates to come out and say a few words."

That's when Phil's pride started raising its poor battered head again. Being such a big man in town he just couldn't afford to have a $200-a-month policeman ordering him around.

"Well, Reverend," he said real brittle like, "I certainly appreciate the invitation but I won't be able to make it!"

"Well, Brother Phil," Delbert drawled, "if you ain't out here in twenty minutes I guess maybe we'll have to conduct the services at your place. Maybe Sister Kathleen would like to say a few words about Sister Rita herself."

That must've brought Phil about three feet off the floor because Sister Kathleen was his wife. He said real quick that on second thought he could make it after all.

Delbert hung up and I guess I should have reprimanded him but when you're rendering unto Caesar you got to speak a language that Caesar understands. And it was the same way with Sam Bates. When Delbert called him, he tried acting like it was Nora Benson, the morphine addict, calling to get him to open up his drugstore and fill a prescription for her.

"Nora," he snarled, when Delbert told him to come on out, "you must have lost your mind. I ain't about to come down there."

"Well," Delbert said, "I'll bring the prescription out to your house then. When you hear a siren, don't be alarmed, it'll just be old Nora."

With that, Sam decided he would open up for old Nora after all. So, while we were waiting on them, Delbert dug the bullets out of the wall and checked for more clues and I called Rita's sister down in Florida and, as gently as I could, I told her what had happened. She seemed to be a milder type girl than Rita and didn't get all mad like I thought she would, just sad.

She said that she had been afraid something like that might happen to Rita and then she said that Rita had mentioned in her letters what a friend I had been to her and would I please have the body shipped down and take care of things until she could come up after the funeral?

I told her I would and for her not to worry, so that took care of that sad business. Then Delbert and I went out on the patio and started discussing the case. It was pretty hard discussing at first because Delbert was so busy gloating over the diary and talking about how he was gonna scare the hell out of this fellow and that fellow and how the citizenry was through addressing him as "hey, you." It was either gonna be "Officer Tate" or "Assistant Chief Tate, sir."

But finally I got him back to the case and we both decided that Dr. Winston wasn't in the clear by a long ways, and we would have to check him out, but Kip, like Oscar said, seemed like our man. One other thing that made it look bad for him was that he hadn't already showed up. He just loved to play Police Commissioner and usually, whenever there was a murder or some sort of excitement, he would always show up with his siren blowing and his pearl-handled pistol showing—neither one of which he was supposed to have—and start bossing the investigation. But this time we hadn't heard a word from him even though Lacey and Pert must have told him about it when they got back from church. Everybody else in town seemed to know about it because, from Rita's back lawn, you could look up the hill and see people stopping their cars to see what was going on.

"But you know what he'll probably say?" Delbert said. "He'll probably say that he slept all morning and that Lacey came home from church and told him about the murder but insisted on her usual after-church loving so he had to take her to bed and then she wouldn't let him go."

Well, Delbert was the best friend I had and I could be pretty frank with him so I told him that I had had enough nasty talk for one morning and if he didn't stop it I was going to shake him worse than I had shook Dr. Winston. That made him real apologetic but it didn't stop him from talking nasty.

He said that he was just saying what Kip would *probably* say. "Personally," he went on, "I don't believe a word he says about Lacey. He's always telling his cronies what a good romp in the hay she is and how that cold, frosty look of hers is just put on and how he has to go home about three afternoons a week for matinees but I just don't believe it.

"If a man's wife wants that much loving he ain't going around talking about it because he knows that some of his friends will decide that he's being overworked and try to give him a hand with it. Besides, if things are that good at Kip's house why's he drinking a fifth of whisky every day and running after Rita and them mattress jockeys down in Mill Town?"

Well, I could have explained every bit of that to him but I didn't. I just tried to shut him up and he did shut up about Lacey for a while but he kept talking about how rotten Kip was and for about the twentieth time he told me about Kip and Nat Rankin.

Nat was a nice, simple, young fellow who worked at the Belton Cooperage Works, the big plant that Kip's daddy had left him. Well, Nat's wife, Mamie, was a wild, pretty, empty-headed young thing and was always making a play for Nat's friends, but out of respect for Nat they wouldn't mess with her.

But Kip heard poor, innocent Nat bragging around the plant about how sweet and pretty Mamie was so he put him on the night shift and took Mamie out to a motel and had relations with her. Now that was bad enough but a couple of days later poor Nat got a package through the mail containing the pants that Mamie had wore that night and with them was an anonymous note saying that Mamie had bounced clean out of 'em.

Well, thanks to Kip having told all his cronies about the cute trick he had pulled, Nat found out it was him and was going to kill him and, if I hadn't been afraid that Kip would kill him first, I might have let him try it. Instead, I talked him out of it and got him a job with a friend of Mr. Phelps's down in Florida.

Of course, Delbert made the story a little more lurid than it was but it was still typical of the things that Kip pulled on people and Delbert said that a man that would do such a thing and tell his friends all sorts of intimate details about his own wife would do anything. "And he done this, Buck!"

It was a comforting thought but I couldn't relish it long because Delbert started preaching at me for not marrying Lacey myself. He said that everybody, knew she wanted to marry me but just because I was a river boy and she belonged to the Greenhill aristocracy I had thought she was too good for me and she had finally give up and married Kip Belton for his money.

"You just treated her too much like a queen," he kept on, "and you still do. Every time she looks at you, you get a look on your face like somebody is giving you an ice water enema."

I told him there wasn't a word of truth in what he was saying but he said there was, too, and that since Lacey had married Kip I had even started acting like I was scared of him. Then he said that he just didn't understand me, that I was a football hero and a war hero and all the people in town, especially the old ladies, thought I was Jesus, Jr., but I just didn't take advantage of my opportunities.

"You could give me that diary," he said, "and we could live in luxury off its contents for the rest of our days." And he had it all figured out. We could make Charley Few, the construction man, build us a camp on the river and make Phil Gaunt keep it stocked with groceries and Sam Bates with whisky, and Hook Phillips with women, and every time we felt a little run down we could just whistle for Dr. Winston and some vitamin pills. "Ain't any man ever gave up as much for his religion as you, Buck."

And he was about to develop that but he was interrupted by Phil Gaunt roaring up in the side yard in his yellow Cadillac and Sam Bates roaring up right behind him in his pink one. They got out looking like a couple of kings that had been summoned to give a command performance before the court clowns. They saw me and Delbert sitting out on the patio and Phil started getting all red and purple and Sam, who's a tall, thin, wormy looking man, started getting a light blue, and then they charged over to give a demonstration of what high esteem the law in Greenhill enjoyed.

"You lint-head sonofabitch," Sam roared at Delbert. "Don't you *ever* call me again. Just what do you think you were doing?"

Phil lit on me. He said I was the one to blame. "You *let* that trashy-mouth sonofabitch call us up. I thought you were our friend, Buck Peters!"

Well, before I could quiet them down Delbert had bounced to his feet and lit on them. He said that if they ever called him anything but Officer Tate and me anything but Chief Peters they were going to have so many stitches in their scalps they would look like they had basketballs for heads.

Then he brought up the matter of them calling me their friend. He said that I had always been a friend to them but they had never been friends to me. They had always treated me like I was a big, dumb dog and all they had to do was whistle and I would come running.

"That's all over!' he said. "That boy is, as of this day, the Angel Gabriel and when he blows his horn *you* come running and you come running hat in hand."

That baffled them more than it scared 'em because Delbert, on my orders, had always been polite and respectful to them before.

"What's this idiot talking about?" Sam snarled, backing away from him. "He's gone crazy."

"Show 'em the horn, Gabriel!" Delbert said. "Blow on it."

Well, he was referring to Rita's diary but I didn't want to use it, so I told them that Delbert was joking, just like he had been joking over the phone, and that all we wanted was for them to answer a few questions about what had happened out at Rita's the night before.

That threw them into another uproar. Phil said that Delbert hadn't been joking, that he had called him "fat butt," and that he wasn't answering any questions about Rita because he hadn't been near her.

"I'm leaving!" he said.

"And so am I!" Sam said.

"Show them the horn!" Delbert said.

"What horn?" Phil bellowed. "You keep talking about a damn horn!"

"This horn!" Delbert sneered and yanked Rita's diary out of my coat pocket. "It's Rita's diary, she left it to Buck, and with the music in this thing, we can blow half the men in this town right into divorce court or Greenhill Cemetery, so you just put your little fat butt down on that chair and start talking!"

"Her diary!" Phil gasped.

"He's lying!" Sam said.

"Well, go right ahead and leave," Delbert told him, "but when you go home go in on your tiptoes because your wife will be on the phone and I'll be reading her page eighty-seven of this Doomsday Book."

That froze him in his tracks and while I didn't bother to tell him that Delbert hadn't seen inside the diary I did tell him that we didn't want to use it to force anybody into co-operating unless we had to.

"Not that I'm suggesting there's anything bad in here about y'all."

"Oh, no!" Delbert cackled. "Nothing *bad*. It's real cute!"

Well, Delbert didn't get that fiendish cackle out good before they were both sitting down sweating and lying about what had happened the night before. It was one of those layer-cake lies. Sam would put on one layer and then Phil would put on another. Sam said they had come out to Rita's the night before all right but it wasn't to throw any party, it was just to take old Clyde Mansfield home. Phil said that was right, that Clyde had got drunk at the Country Club Stag and announced that he was going to put on an exhibition of his sexual powers at Rita's and everybody was invited.

"Him being seventy-three though," Sam said, "we naturally figured he was joking, but the next time we looked around he was gone so we figured maybe he had come out here so we came out to look for him."

"Yeah," said Phil, "and there he was on the lawn out there beating on his bony old chest like a sex mad skeleton and challenging Rita to let him in."

"So," Sam said, "we put him in the car and took him home and then we went home ourselves and that's all in God's world that happened!"

"Every bit of it," Phil said. "Yet just because we save an old man from disgracing himself we get hounded like common criminals."

I looked at Delbert and he looked at Phil. "Phil," he said, "you just *think* you been hounded. You tell one more lie like that one and you're gonna feel like Uncle Tom."

That set 'em off again and they wanted to know just what we meant by accusing them of lying so I told them about my talk with Chastain at the Police Station that morning and how Chastain had said that Kip Belton had broken up a drunken party at Rita's around eleven o'clock.

That broke their spirits again and Phil started in on another lie but with a little more of the truth creeping into it. He said that they had been at the Stag at the Club and after the dirty film had been shown they all decided that they would come out to Rita's and serenade her, as a joke sort of. However, when they got in the car Clyde Mansfield and Charlie Few had started arguing about who was the greatest lover and they decided they would try and persuade Rita to let them settle the issue under actual battle conditions.

"But," Sam broke in, "Phil and I were horrified at the thought of such crudeness and tried to stop them but they outvoted us. Dink Tompkins and Tom Bagshaw were in the car with us too."

"I see," said Delbert, real prissy like. "A whole carload of leading citizens, all of you disgustingly drunk."

"Me and Phil hadn't had a drink!" Sam said.

"That makes it worse!" Delbert said. "You and Phil come out here stark sober and let four drunks try to put on a revolting exhibition with a dear girl that..."

Well, right then Phil must have figured it was every man for himself. "I wasn't sober," he said. "I was dead drunk. I don't remember a thing that happened!"

"Well, that's merciful!" Sam snapped right back. "You were the one that went up and beat on Rita's door."

"I never stirred once," Phil said. "Clyde was the one who beat on the door but when Rita come to the door in her negligee you let out a nasty whoop and ran up the walk and told Clyde to never mind, that you would take over."

"That's a lie! All I did was sit in the car and blow the horn for y'all to come on and let's go home!"

I could see we weren't getting anywhere that way, so I just put my foot down and told them that we knew for certain that they had all been in Rita's house throwing a party but we didn't care about that. "What we want to know," I said, "is what happened after Kip ran you off."

"Yeah," said Delbert, "according to what Kip told Chastain y'all got mad at him and Rita both and somebody in the crowd mumbled something about coming back and wrecking the place. Now just who came back?"

Well, that brought them both to their feet. "Kip Belton said that *we* said *we* were coming back and wreck the place?" Sam snorted.

He hadn't told Chastain any such thing, of course, but since we were trying to protect Oscar I let Delbert keep on.

"That's exactly what he said," Delbert said. "And Chastain rode past here about three forty-five and he saw you driving off and he thinks maybe you're the one that ..."

That took the cork out of the jug. Sam let out a roar and said, "Oh no, by damn, they don't! They ain't making a patsy out of Sam Bates! Not for any murder!"

And with that he started in and this time it was the truth with all the trimmings. He said that after the showing of the dirty films at the club around ten o'clock they had come out to

Rita's and done some whooping and hollering but she hadn't minded it, instead she had got tickled at old Clyde and invited them in for a drink.

"And we were having a nice, wholesome time," Sam said. "We were drinking and singing and laughing at Clyde and Rita. She'd been monogramming a sheet and Clyde had put it on and wrapped a vine, from one of her potted plants, around his head and was claiming that he was Julius Caesar and she was his little Cleopatra. Then, just as he was raving about what a pretty asp she had, that bastard Belton came busting through the door.

"He was roaring nasty drunk but we tried being nice to him and even invited him to join the party, but he wanted Rita all to himself so he claimed that the police had had a complaint about all the hell we were raising and he had come out to put a stop to it.

"Well, that didn't make any impression at all on Clyde because he was so drunk that he thought he really was Julius Caesar, and he got real regal and wanted to know where that big fat eunuch had come from, meaning Kip, and then he ordered us to feed him to the lions. Well, Rita got to laughing, and the more she laughed the madder Kip got, and he started roaring that he was the Police Commissioner and if we didn't get that dirty old man out of the house in sixty seconds he was going to arrest the whole bunch of us!"

"And we hadn't done a damn thing to be arrested for," Phil broke in, "but we didn't want to have any trouble with that maniac so we all grabbed Clyde and drug him outside, but as we were driving off he started blubbering and babbling in some sort of strange tongue and finally we figured out what he was telling us was to stop the car, that he had lost his teeth.

"And he had. I ran my finger around in his mouth to see if he was lying, but there wasn't a sign of a tooth, and I figured they'd dropped out when we had to bring him out of the house upside down and he hadn't realized it till he got right side up. But we didn't want any more trouble with Kip so Sam parked but on the road and we told the rest of 'em to hold on to Clyde and the two of us came back to look for Clyde's teeth."

"And that's when it happened," Sam said. "We sneaked back down here and found Clyde's teeth in the flower bed by the steps and I was dusting the dirt and the manure off of 'em and Phil was taking a peek in the living-room window to see what Kip was doing. Well, he took a peek and then he rushed over and told me that Kip was dragging Rita down the hall and was gonna rape her it looked like.

"So we rushed around to Rita's bedroom window and, sure enough, Kip was wrestling with her and trying to force her down on the bed and telling her that she had put him off long enough. Well, we would've gone in to help her but all of a sudden she didn't act mad any more.

"She started laughing and told Kip that she guessed she had teased him long enough but at least let her get her nightgown off. Well, his eyes lit up like he had stuck his toe in a wall socket and he turned her loose and started smirking that couldn't any of 'em resist old Belton. That smirk lasted just long enough for Rita to turn her back on him and reach into the drawer of her night table and get her pistol."

"And she was just itching to use it on him," Phil said. "She jammed it in that big belly of his clean up to the trigger guard, and started calling him the filthiest names you ever heard and then when he started whimpering and backing away, she started sneering at him for thinking he was a ladies' man.

"She told him that the only way he ever got a woman or a friend or anything else was with the money his daddy had left him and if it wasn't for that he'd be another Stool Williams only she had more respect for Stool."

Well, poor Stool Williams was the village idiot and I could see what was coming because, if there was one thing Kip couldn't stand, it was somebody reminding him that he'd never done a thing on his own in his life and that if it wasn't for his daddy's money and the plant he had left him he wouldn't be any Police Commissioner, he wouldn't be in society, he wouldn't be anything but a bum.

"So," Phil said, "when she put that gun on him and gave him that character reading and sneered about him being a great lover, he got crazy, crying mad and started screaming that he was going to come back and rape her or kill her one."

"And that's just what the sonofabitch did," Sam snarled, "and he ain't making me his pigeon. We didn't see him do it, he must've come back after we left, but *he's* the one who done it, not *us!*"

That was all I had hoped for but Delbert had to give the knife a final twist.

"So," he sneered, "you peeping-toms hung around a while and then left, but you never thought of reporting it to the police."

Well, Sam knew we had him in our power but he just couldn't pass that up. "Report it to the police! The way Buck bows and scrapes to Belton, what the hell good would it have done?" Then he turned on me and whined, "You've hounded us, by God, now let's see you hound him!"

"Yeah!" Phil said. "You hound us and we never did you a harm in the world but you won't hound him and he stole your girl. You're scared of both of 'em. If you ain't, go on out there!"

CHAPTER FOUR

LACEY AND I fell into one another's clutches when we were both sixteen. It was on a sunny Saturday morning in April and, as usual, I was on the river. I had been fishing, sitting on this big sycamore that sloped out over the water, and I had hung a big catfish and it had run to the bottom and wrapped the line around a root. But I knew he hadn't broken off because I could still feel him, every now and then, pumping against the line.

So I had peeled off all my clothes and gone down after him. It was about twelve foot of water and I had to make three trips down but I got him. I cooned him through the gills and then fought my way back to the surface. He was a blue and weighed six pounds and was the biggest cat I'd ever caught on a hand-line.

Then, after I got him staked out on my stringer, I climbed back up onto the sycamore and sat there basking naked in the sun and watching my fish swimming and bucking about two foot below the surface. I must have sat there basking and watching for about ten minutes but all of a sudden I wasn't enjoying myself any more. I had the feeling of being watched. What was worse, though, was the thought that somebody had found my spot.

It was on a real wild, dense, wooded section of the river where you would expect the ground under the trees to be all muck and overgrown with snake grass and swamp ivy and poison oak but this place wasn't.

It was a clearing in the trees about thirty foot square that you couldn't see from the river because there was a whole line of willows shielding it. The morning sun could get to it and the whole clearing was covered with a regular carpet of wild, thick, soft grass. It was the prettiest spot I'd ever found on the river and never visited by anybody but me because I'd never found any beer cans or whisky bottles or sardine cans around. So naturally I couldn't help being upset at the thought of somebody else finding it.

I didn't move, though. I just sat there like I was meditating but all the time I was checking the trees and the bushes for movement. Then I heard a sound in the willows just a little piece up from me. Then it came again, like something had lodged in the willows and was being pushed down by the current. Then I saw what it was. It was a green canoe. I could just see the front of it but it had the initials *M.J.S.* on it and I knew whose it was, Mr. Martin Satterfield's.

Mr. Satterfield was a real nice fellow who lived in Greenhill but had a cottage on the river about a half mile up from where my mother and I lived. But the main reason I knew it was his boat was that his niece, Lacey Satterfield, was always coming out from town and using it. She would come paddling by the house and, if I was on the front porch, she would always holler up and ask me if I didn't want to go with her.

I always wanted to go but I never had. I was in the same class with her at Greenhill High and, even though everybody was making a lot of my ball playing and being real nice to me so I wouldn't drop out of school and go to work, I just never could feel at ease around her. For one thing, I had always liked hunting and fishing so much that I'd never messed around with girls but the main reason was that Lacey was so pretty and so overpowering sort of that every time she'd talk to me I'd come down with some kind of lover's lockjaw and wouldn't be able to do anything but get red and mumble and go hunh.

At any rate, that's how I knew it was Mr. Satterfield's boat. I figured it had just got loose from his dock during the night and had drifted down the river. So I jumped down into the water and towed it back down to the sycamore and started to sun myself some more, but all of a sudden I *knew* I was being watched. I glanced back into the clearing real quick and I never got such a shock. There, sitting right on top of my clothes, was Lacey Satterfield.

I just fell off that tree into the water, but as cold as it was it still didn't convince me I wasn't dreaming. Lacey Satterfield just wouldn't sit and smile at a boy who was stark naked. She wouldn't because my mother had always said the Satterfields were the nicest people in Greenhill. They may have lost all their money but they were still quality—you could tell by the way they treated people. And Lacey was as nice as any Satterfield. She might be high-spirited and like to shock people with some of her forward ideas but it was always people who needed a shock.

So after I threw myself into the water and came up, I stared up into the clearing knowing that Lacey wouldn't be there. But there she was. She wasn't smiling any more, she was biting her lip trying to keep from laughing.

"Come on out, Buck!" she said.

As usual, I couldn't think of anything to say, but when she stood up and started coming down to the water I said something then. I said, "No!" as loud as I could and started swimming downriver. She tried following me but the clearing was walled in by vines trailing down from the trees so she stopped and started laughing.

"You'd just as well come back!" she called out. "You can't go home without your clothes and I'm going to sit on them until you do come back."

I didn't think I was dreaming then, I thought I was going crazy. She just couldn't be meaning what she was saying because what she was saying was that she wanted to see me naked. I swam about thirty yards farther down to a muscadine vine trailing in the water and then pulled myself up on the bank and started back through the trees toward the clearing. There were so many vines that she didn't have a chance of seeing me, so I got up the nerve to holler.

"Lacey?"

She hollered right back, "Yes, Buck!"

I really had a horrible thought then. *I* hadn't gone crazy. *She* had gone crazy. She was president of our class at school, she was president of our class at Sunday School and she always sang "O Little Town of Bethlehem" at Christmas services. But she had stalked me down the river, sneaked up on me, captured my clothes and was sitting out in the clearing waiting to see me naked. She *had* to be crazy. I never felt so sorry for anybody in my life.

"Lacey," I called out. "You need help!"

She just laughed. "No, *you* need help!" Then she said she would make a bargain with me. "I'll bring your clothes halfway, Buck, and then come back here while you dress, but you've got to promise me that you'll come back and talk to me as long as I want to talk. Is that a bargain?"

Well, I wanted my clothes back so bad that I quit debating who was crazy. "Yes, m'am," I hollered back. "It's a bargain."

That started her laughing again and then I heard her coming through the trees. She was true to her bargain. When I hollered, "That's halfway!" she laughed some more and put my clothes on a stump and went back to the clearing. I flitted from tree to tree until I was even with the stump and then I dashed out and got my clothes and dashed back behind a tree and put them on.

All they amounted to was a pair of overall pants and a blue denim shirt but my hands were shaking so I like to never got them on. Then Lacey called out again.

"Buck, are you decent?"

I buttoned up the front of my britches and gave my hair a swipe and said that I was. She said, all right, come on out and keep my part of the bargain. Well, I started for her and halfway to the clearing I wasn't shaking so much. Then, when I went a little further, I started getting mad. The closer to the clearing, the madder I got. Lacey Satterfield might be quality to my mother but she sure wasn't to me and I was going to tell her so.

By that time I was right up to the vines and the trees bordering the clearing. I still couldn't see her but I knew she was there so I started through.

"Lacey Satterfield," I said, "I want to talk to you!"

"You'd *better* talk to me!" she called out. "You made me a solemn promise you'd talk to me just as long as I wanted to talk."

"I know it," I said, fighting my way through the vines, "and that's just what I'm going to do."

"You swear it?" she said.

"I sure do swear it," I said, and with that I busted through the vines into the clearing. That one maneuver changed my whole life. Lacey Satterfield, President of the Young People for Christ Sunday School Class, was standing right out in the middle of the clearing without a stitch of clothes on.

For about thirty seconds I just gave up. I *had* to be going crazy. The most I'd ever seen of any girl was down at the Greenhill swimming pool and all I'd seen then—not that I was looking for it—was about twelve inches of thigh and a little bare chest and shoulder. But now I was eight miles out on the river and the nicest girl in town was standing right in front of me stark, raving naked.

Like I say, for about thirty seconds, I just stood there staring. But, with the Lord as my witness, I wasn't thinking any evil thoughts. For one thing my brain was numb and for another thing I just had the strange feeling all over that it wasn't really evil. She was standing there with her arms folded—but not. hiding anything—smiling at me just as though I was her brother and we were getting ready to play a game of mumbledy-peg or something like that.

At least that's the way it looked at first. Her hair was even blonder then and the sun was giving it a soft, silver glimmer like milkweed that's burst from its pod and her breasts weren't anything like I thought breasts were. I'd seen some fat girls down at the swimming pool who sort of lapped over out of their suits but they just made me sick and Delbert had brought a dirty cartoon book to school—I didn't know it was dirty when I looked—and the women in it had even worse breasts than the fat girls, but Lacey's weren't that way at all. Hers, well, they must have looked just the way the Lord meant for them to look because they didn't make you think evil at all. They just gave you a sort of satisfied feeling like when you see a good job of carpentering or brick laying and you know it's done right according to plans and a lot of good, careful work has gone into it.

And the rest of her gave me the same sort of feeling. In that same book Delbert had, there was this coarse picture of a naked woman and her hips were all big and blubbery and the rest of her was even more of a mess. Of course I knew the picture wasn't true to life but I never dreamed that a girl could be put together as trim and neat and tidy as Lacey. Her legs and her hips and her chest were tapered just right and curved right into one another without any knobby bones or rolls of fat to break it up and her stomach was just as flat as a board and even the rest of her was a pleasant surprise too.

But when I realized I was thinking all those thoughts and that my brain wasn't numb any more and that my eyes were even glorying in what they saw, I started getting panic struck again. Not that I was abnormal or anything like that. I was having awful dreams about girls at that time of my life and whenever Lacey would sit behind me at chapel and lean over and tell me something and breathe on my neck I would just about die. It was just that this was all so sudden and so against everything I'd been taught.

My mother was one of the most unbending Christians that ever lived and every night she would read me a chapter out of the Bible and I don't think a one of 'em ever had a happy ending.

They were all about thieves and fornicators and they all went to hell wholesale and suffered all sorts of tortures, and I was given to understand that the same could be in store for me only more so because I'd been warned.

Lacey must have been able to read my mind and known that I was getting ready to run because she just smiled and crooked her finger for me to come closer. "If you don't," she grinned, "I'll scream and Dernie Stokes will hear me. He's just up the river."

Well, I found out later Dernie wasn't up the river but it stopped me from running then. He was a big, tough, commercial fisherman who was real fond of the Satterfields, and if he found Lacey naked and screaming he would kill me on the spot. So there wasn't anything for me to do but shuffle out into the clearing with her. She made me come so close that I broke out in goose flesh or heat rash one and then she started stating her business and it was kind of what I had a feeling it would be. It was sex.

She said that she knew that nice girls weren't supposed to think about sex but she thought that was stupid because you couldn't help thinking about it and could wreck your mind trying not to. Or something like that. I was so nervous that anything that took any thought was just over my head.

But then she got to talking plain. She said that she had overheard a lot of talk in the cloakroom at school about sex and she had read it in novels but there was so much difference between what she had heard and what she had read that she didn't know what to believe, so she was going to find out for herself. If it was as ugly and as cheap as it sounded in the cloakroom she was going to forget about it and wouldn't lie awake any more nights wondering. If it was as beautiful as it sounded in the books, though, that would be different.

"But I'm not going to be tormented about it any longer, Buck Peters. You are going to be my lover!"

I couldn't run. She'd scream and bring Dernie, I thought. So I just stood there gaping at her while she explained why she had picked me. She said it wasn't because I was a football hero or the best-looking boy in the class or anything like that. It was because I was such a nice, Christian boy and she knew I never would say a word about what had happened.

Now as confused as I was I could see that that didn't make any sense and I started telling her that she didn't really think I was a nice, Christian boy or she'd know I wasn't going to do such a thing. And I told her I wasn't just a nice boy, I was a scared boy, and if I did what she wanted me to, we would both go straight to hell and my mother could quote her Bible verses all day long proving it.

"All right, Buck Peters," she snapped, "if you won't be my lover, I'll get Kip Belton."

That was all she needed to say. Just the thought of it made me sick and she saw that it did and, even worse, she realized how much I loved her and how she could make me do anything she wanted. She looked like she felt real sorry for me but the threat never left her lips.

"You know what will happen then, don't you?" she said. "Kip will tell it all over town just like he does when he goes out with those Mill Town girls."

I could just see Kip parked out in front of Bates Pharmacy in his red convertible telling his drooling cronies all about it. And Lacey knew I was having visions like that because she smiled up at me full of triumph and evil and started unbuttoning my shirt and asking me if I had ever been Edie Fulmer's lover.

Edie lived on the river just above us and had a reputation for carrying on with everybody. My eyes answered that question for Lacey too. I had never even kissed a girl except playing Post Office and Spin the Bottle at a couple of parties.

That made Lacey's smile even more evil and she started sort of caressing my chest as she undid my shirt and the next thing I knew she had all the buttons undone and had slid the shirt off my shoulders. Then she started breathing a little faster and looked up at me with her eyes even shinier and started unbuttoning my pants. I couldn't help putting my hands down to keep them from falling but she told me to put them around her or she would scream. So I put them around her waist and held them as loose as I could. Then I felt my pants down around my ankles and then I was kicking my feet loose.

And right then was when Lacey trapped us both forever. She reached up and put her arms around my neck and kissed me and started pressing herself to me. I could feel her breasts against my chest and her stomach against mine and the whole world changed. It was like I had been real cold and scared and somebody all of a sudden had turned a hose of real warm water on me and washed away all the cold and the fright and everything that had caused it.

I just wasn't myself any more. At least not my real self. I was the Buck Peters in those dreams I had about girls. I had wings on my feet and honey in my veins and the whole world was warm and soft and wonderful and going to be even more that way. I was just all of a sudden depraved. My own mother could have beat me on the back and told me to put my clothes on and I would have just laughed at her.

And Lacey seemed to feel the same way. She pressed herself closer to me and started breathing real fast and then she was making us one and that was when the trouble all started. She tensed up and said in a halfgasp, "Buck, no!"

Well, I heard her but I felt so warm and nice and lovable that I just couldn't believe she really meant it, so I just pulled her closer....

"I'll tell your mother, Buck!" she screamed. "You'll go to hell!"

She couldn't make me believe it. I was a sweet honey bee and she was a golden buttercup, I was a little sunbeam and she was a sleeping morning glory.

All of a sudden she wasn't screaming any more and, instead of trying to push me away, she had her arms about me pulling me closer....

Then my feet fell off. At least that's the way it felt. They didn't fall off all at once, just gradually. Then when they fell all the way off, my whole life felt like it was oozing away. And then I fainted.

At least I came awfully close to fainting or I went into a coma or something. I didn't know anything for a while and then I was lying on my back in the clearing and Lacey was standing over me with her hands on her hips, glaring at me like she wanted to kill me. I didn't know what to make of it. I just blinked up at her and then everything started coming back. I wasn't any sweet honey bee, I wasn't any sunbeam, I was a monster.

I tried telling myself it hadn't happened, that I couldn't have been that depraved, but there she was, her chest heaving and tears glittering in her eyes and trying to think of something bad enough to call me. The next thing I knew I was on my knees with my arms clasped around her, crying and begging her forgiveness.

For what seemed like forever she just stood there, then she reached down and grabbed my by the hair and forced my head back so I'd have to look up at her in all my shame. The tears in her eyes started getting bigger and brighter and then they were brimming over and falling on to my own cheeks and each one of 'em burning a hole in my sorry, black soul. But every tear that fell seemed to drain away a little of the hate in her eyes and pretty soon there wasn't any hate in them at all, just a bright, shiny look of forgiveness.

I rose and gathered her up in my arms like she was a little child and took her down to the river and bathed the tears from her cheeks and the grass stains from her hips and her elbows and dried her with my shirt and carried her back to the clearing and sat her down in the shade of a willow. Then I reached over and got her blouse and started to put it on her but she just looked at me with a soft, shiny look in her eyes and I made it into a little cushion for her to sit on.

I thought then that we'd talk, but she just kept looking at me and to save myself I couldn't think of anything to say that I hadn't already said in my plea for forgiveness, so I went down to my boat. Mama had put me up some fried chicken and hard-boiled eggs and melon pickles for lunch. I got the sack and the fruit jar of lemonade and brought it all back to Lacey and spread out the newspaper that the jar had been wrapped in and put the lunch on it.

She still didn't say anything or even move, so I tore a strip of white meat from the chicken breast and held it out to her and she smiled and took a bite of it from my fingers. I put the lemonade to her lips and she drank and the whole meal was like that and I was grateful to her for it because I felt like a monster being allowed to make up to a little girl he had hurt but hadn't meant to.

For a whole hour, I guess, I felt like a monster. When the chicken and everything was gone I went down to the river and wet my bandana and came back and bathed her lips and her hands and then she started doing the same to me. And when she started that I began to realize that I wasn't any monster, I was just a poor, innocent, little boy playing nursemaid to a tiger.

I first noticed it when she started cleaning the chicken grease off my hand. She didn't scrub my hand, she stroked it. Then she'd gone beyond my hand and dropped the bandana and was stroking my arm, caressing it sort of. I started feeling like a snake being charmed. Her hand moved from my arm to my chest and then across my chest up over my shoulder and then joined fingers with a hand I didn't even know was there. Then I thought I was going crazy again. Her lips were at my ear and she was sighing, "Love me, Buck. Love me again!"

I tried getting aloose from her. I tried getting to my feet. I tried telling her that I had sworn an oath to myself that I'd never do anything like that again. But her arms were around my neck and I was off balance and the next thing I knew I was on my back and she was on me.

But I couldn't have looked down at her as evil as she was looking down at me. Her eyes were just dancing with evil and so was her smile and she was saying that I *would so* love her again. I would love her whenever she said and wherever she said and as long as she said or she would have me killed. She would tell her Uncle Martin that I had raped her and he would take her to Dr. Hackett and he would see that I had and he would spread the word around and before sundown I would be lynched and hanging from the limb of some tree with my poor mother clinging to my feet and sobbing.

Well, for the sake of my dear mother there wasn't a thing I could do but give in to Lacey. I took the oath that I would do anything she wanted, whenever and wherever she wanted it done. But I warned her that my heart wasn't going to be in it because my love for her was pure and good and not of the flesh but the soul.

She just smiled her slow evil smile and then her mouth was on mine. And later she was lying with her head on my chest talking to me. She said that no matter what happened she would never love anybody but me and, because of my oath, I couldn't afford to ever love anybody but her.

Then finally, way down the river, we heard the 4:40 train crossing the trestle and Lacey kissed me and pulled me to my feet and said that we had better be going because I was going to have supper with her and Uncle Martin. I just sighed and started helping her on with her blouse, that's how much she had me cowed and broke in spirit and in love with her.

We went back in my boat and towed the canoe. I was so weak and spent I'd have to stop and rest about every half mile and then Lacey would laugh and get on the seat beside me and take an oar and we'd row along together. That's the way we went past home. Mama was on the front porch and Lacey hollered up and told her that I was having supper with them. Mama looked real surprised at first but then she looked real pleased and said it was mighty nice of Lacey asking me. I just thanked the Lord that she didn't inquire as to what had made me so weak that I had to have a girl help me row.

Lacey's Uncle Martin was on his dock, fishing. He was a tall, handsome, white-haired man and real educated but he always spoke nice to everybody and everybody liked him although they thought he was a little odd for spending so much of his time hunting and fishing instead of trying to get even with the Beltons for what they had done to the Satterfields.

Anyway, when he saw us coming rowing up, he acted real pleased to see me. But when we got closer to the dock and he saw how bright and spirited and talky Lacey was and how tired and wore out I was, his expression sort of changed. He still looked pleased but he looked puzzled too.

But he never said what he was puzzled about. Going up to the cottage from the dock, though, I noticed how close he was studying us. He was talking about how he wanted me to play football for the college he'd gone to but his mind was more on me and Lacey. He was noticing how Lacey was hugging my arm as we walked along and how I looked like I didn't know whether I was going to get myself up the hill, much less both of us.

Then, when we got to the cottage and Lacey went in to fix supper, he told me to stay out on the porch with him that he wanted to talk to me. Well, that scared me nearly to death but all he did was start talking more football. But then, when he had me all relaxed and off guard, he all of a sudden changed the subject and said real casual like, "Well, Buck, what did you and Lacey do today?"

There wasn't a thing I could do to stop it. My face started getting red and then redder and I felt like my whole head was going to bust into flames. Then I leaned forward and said, "What'd you say, Mr. Martin?" That's when my face got reddest of all. I had tried to sound real casual too and keep my voice steady, but instead I just croaked it out.

For about five seconds he didn't say a word. In place of the puzzled look in his eyes there was a sort of amazed look like he had found out what he wanted to know but couldn't believe it. And Lacey made it worse. She probably had been listening to everything, because right at that point she flounced out on the porch and sat on the floor right at my feet and looked up at me and started gushing.

"Uncle Martin," she said, "I've decided that Buck is going to be my sweetheart. All the other boys at school want to neck all the time but Buck isn't that way at all. He just likes to go out in the woods and fish and swim and lie in the sun and talk about God and Jesus. Isn't that right, Buck?"

My face couldn't get any redder without it bleeding, so I just started slipping further and further down in the chair and by the time she was through I was almost on my back looking like a corpse all laid out.

But maybe it saved me from being a corpse. Mr. Martin was almost certain by then what had happened and this rage started coming into his eyes but then he saw how shamed I was and how Lacey was torturing me and he couldn't help knowing that it had all been her idea. Then he had to fight to keep his face straight so he wouldn't bust out laughing.

That wasn't all, though. Lacey turned around, looked up at him, and then, in this voice that wasn't soft and sweet and gushy any more, she said, "I've got it all figured out, Uncle Martin. I'll marry Kip Belton first, I'll get all the Satterfield money back from the Beltons, I'll make Kip as miserable as his daddy made mine, and then I'll marry Buck and we'll live happily ever after."

It was Mr. Martin's time to suck in his breath. He was finding out what I already knew. Lacey Satterfield wasn't just a beautiful, high-spirited girl, she was part witch.

CHAPTER FIVE

WELL, sir, neither Sam Bates nor Phil Gaunt nor anybody else had any idea about my true relationship with Lacey past or present nor did they know that I wasn't in awe of Kip Belton or his money or his position or anything else. I did indulge him and let him treat me pretty shabby at times but it was only because I was a Christian, and a Christian has to atone for everything evil he does in his life, so that was my way of atoning for having relations with his wife. If you're going to be nice to a man's wife, the least you can do is be nice to him too.

Besides, it was my official duty to see that he paid for his sins in full, which could mean that I might even have to shoot him some day, and I didn't think it would be very smart policemanship putting him on notice. Not that I was being sneaky. After all, when Gideon was after the Midianites, he didn't go blowing any trumpets or busting any lamps until he had the drop on them, and Kip was worse than any Midianite.

But, not knowing what I was up to, Sam Bates and Phil Gaunt had managed to work themselves up into another rage and there they were on Rita's patio accusing me of being afraid to hound Kip the way I had hounded them.

"Let this garbage-mouth bastard call him like he did us!" Sam said, meaning Delbert.

"Yeah!" said Phil. "Call him a fat butt!"

"We will," said Delbert, ripping off another one of his lies, "just as soon as we get through talking to that fellow from the Memphis paper. He's on his way out."

That scared them even worse than Rita's diary had because almost everybody in town took a Memphis paper. Sam's eyes bugged out and he gave this gasp: "A reporter?"

"And a photographer!" Delbert lied. "You and Phil can re-enact that peeping-tom scene for him."

Well, with that Phil started pleading for me to listen to him but I didn't have to because his face told me everything I wanted to know. If I wouldn't tell the reporter about them they never would revile us any more, they never would sell any more whisky at the Country Club on Sunday and they never would show up at any more drunken driving cases and swear that the defendant hadn't had anything but a short beer and a hay fever pill and it was the hay fever pill that made him side-swipe four cars, knock down a telephone pole and get out of the car thinking he was Stonewall Jackson.

So I told them, all right, that if they would cooperate with us, and not say anything to Kip or anybody else about what had happened I would protect them as much as the law allowed. They almost licked my hand.

"Any time you need us, boy," Sam said, "you call us."

"You too, Officer Tate," said Phil. "Any time!"

And with that they almost ran out to their cars and took off in a cloud of gravel and shredded rubber. Delbert turned to me and shook my hand and gloated some more and said that took care of the mice, now for the rat. He meant Kip and right away we had a big argument about how we would handle him. He wanted to take him down to the station and brain-wash him with a rubber hose but I finally convinced him that that was the worst thing we could do. We just didn't have enough proof.

And we didn't. The way Sam and Phil had been talking in that toilet at Sim Everette's café somebody besides Oscar could have overheard them and come out and killed Rita, knowing that the blood would be on Kip's hands.

Dr. Winston could have done it while he was supposed to be at the Clinic waiting on that woman's baby to come. He wasn't the type to sit around a labor room holding an expectant mother's hand and clocking her pains, and he could have slipped down to Sim's for a sandwich, overheard Phil and Sam and slipped out and administered unto Rita himself.

Or old Clyde Mansfield could have sneaked back and done it because he wasn't the old clown he was always acting. He had been Turk Singleton's best friend and he'd sworn that he was going to kill Rita for killing Turk. Of course, he said he was going to kill her the same way she had killed Turk but that was just wishful thinking.

And then there were some women suspects in town, about four or five hundred of 'em. Della Starnes, an old sweetheart of Turk's, had practically tried getting the Golden Rule Bible Class to put a bounty on Rita's head and she lived just up the hill from Rita. She or any of the rest of 'em *could* have done it but Delbert didn't want to admit it.

"Maybe *you* did it!" he said, real disgusted. "You say you were out on the river fishing all night. Maybe you tied up at that old dock at the end of the road and came up here and Rita tried to rape you again and you shot her in self-defense. Now *that* I could believe!"

Well, I hadn't been out on the river all night fishing like I had said. I had been in Kip Belton's garden with Lacey and it was beginning to worry me but I hadn't killed Rita so I let Delbert's humor pass. I started explaining that I thought Kip was the murderer too but, if we let him know we thought so, right away he would start throwing his million dollars around and get himself a city lawyer and start buying up witnesses and alibis.

But, if he didn't know he was the chief suspect, he would just sit tight maybe and we could beat him to the half a dozen or so people in town who might be willing to furnish him with an alibi. There weren't any more than that—a couple of his cronies, a couple of his Mill Town girls and a few fellows like Hook Phillips who ran joints out in the county. Everybody else hated him too much.

We wouldn't ask his cronies and girls about him directly. Instead we would act like we thought they might be involved in the murder themselves and get statements from them about what they were doing around three-thirty and who they were with and who they saw. They would be so busy saving themselves they wouldn't think about Kip and, if none of them mentioned being with him or seeing him, then we would have them on record as saying so, and when alibi time rolled around he would be real hard put. And even if one of them tried to change his story, we would have enough to trip him up.

"But like I say," I told Delbert, "maybe he don't need an alibi. Maybe he was at home in bed at three-thirty. We haven't got any proof that he wasn't so the only thing we can do is sit tight until we find out."

Now Delbert knew that made sense but he wanted to argue and he asked me why I wanted to call Kip at all then. I explained that I was going to call him just to throw him off guard. I would tell him what Chastain had told us about him breaking up the party at Rita's and then I would give him the impression that we thought he had left right after the party too. Not knowing that Sam and them had overheard his threat to Rita, he wouldn't suspect a thing and would just sit tight.

"All right," Delbert sighed, "call him."

So I called his number but that just caused more turmoil because Pert, that beautiful, voluptuous eighteen-year-old sister of his, who was staying with them while her mother was in Europe, answered the phone. When I asked for Kip, she started in tormenting me as usual and asked if I wouldn't rather have her instead. "We've got something to talk about too, Yum-Yum," she said.

Well, she had one of those perfumed, double-meaning voices that could make the Beatitudes sound like the Mann Act and when Delbert, who was listening in, heard her say what she did, he had one of his sex fits and started whinnying and beating on a pillow and kicking the furniture.

She affected him that way. She would come into the Police Station three or four times a week acting like she was looking for Kip, but then she would come back to my desk and start tantalizing me and wanting to know when I was going to take her out.

I would try to be real stern and fatherly with her but she would just grin and lean over my shoulder like she wanted to see the papers on my desk and, even though there wasn't but one of her, I'd feel like it was raining young breasts and soft, black hair and red satin lips and velvet cheeks. It was like having a bucket of love potions dumped over your head.

But it would run Delbert even crazier than it did me and, after she left, he would hoot and holler and butt his head against the wall and ask me what I was waiting for. I would try telling him that she invited my attentions because she knew I was a Christian boy and would decline the invitation, but he'd just keep on slobbering.

Besides, Pert knew how mad her lusting after me made Kip and Lacey and, sure enough, just as soon as she said what she did, Lacey snatched the telephone away from her and told me that little Yum-Yum had just had her hormone shot and I would have to pardon her.

Then she asked me what I wanted and I paused and asked Delbert if he would go outside and see if somebody wasn't walking around the yard, that I thought I heard somebody. It wasn't very subtle but he was so disgusted that he went out to look and as quick as I could I told Lacey about Kip and Rita.

For about five seconds she didn't say a word and I thought Pert must still be in the room but then I rightly figured that such news would naturally leave her speechless. For one thing she knew better than anybody how rotten Kip was but she'd never thought of him as a murderer. For another thing, if he was the murderer, it would mean that he was finally going to get what was coming to him and that her daddy was going to be avenged at last.

"Buck," she murmured finally, "are you positive?"

She was scared to get her hopes up but I convinced her that I wasn't lying, and then I asked her if he had gotten home before three-thirty. She couldn't keep the gloating out of her voice. She said he hadn't come in until four-thirty and he was blind drunk and had banged on her door and, as usual, she hadn't let him in so he had floundered off to his own room. All of which meant that he was afoot when Rita was murdered.

I would have started gloating myself but Delbert came back in and said there wasn't anybody in the yard. Well, then I asked Lacey if I could speak to Kip and she said, no, that he was down by the swimming pool and if I wanted to speak to him I would have to come out there. I thanked her and said I would be out and then I hung up and Delbert started in again. He said that he just couldn't understand how I could call myself a Christian and treat poor, little old Pert the way I did.

"Her little old pants just on fire and her begging you to come put out the blaze but you just as good as tell her to get off the phone!"

Well, I tried explaining that she had said what she did just to make Lacey mad and besides she wasn't but eighteen years old but that just made him howl all the louder. "Well, what the hell do you want? Whistler's Mother? Eighteen years old ain't veal, Buck, it's beef, and you're the butcher and you'd just as well go ahead and butcher her because she ain't going to get off the chopping block till you do!"

Finally I convinced him that it was Kip we were after and not his sister and that we had to move fast because I figured that twenty-four hours was the longest we could keep him unsuspecting. He grumbled all the way back into town and then we picked up my car at the church. He left to contact the people that Kip might try to use as an alibi and I left to contact Kip himself.

He lived on River Road, too, about a mile from Rita's, only on the upper slope instead of the lower one. His daddy had built the house and dirtier money never turned out a prettier place. It was a big, red brick, white-columned mansion sitting at the top of a long sloping lawn that was dotted with dogwoods and bordered by pines.

Due to my relations with Lacey, every time I went up to the house I felt like Jack going up the Bean Stalk but this time I felt a little better, or at least until I pulled around in back and parked just off the terrace and got out and found Pert there waiting for me.

I was just thankful that Delbert wasn't with me because he would have pawed up the whole yard. She had on a pair of white shorts that looked like they had been sprayed on and high heels and one of these halter sort of blouses that was pulled up so tight it would have brought out the numbers on a pool ball. But what disturbed me even more than the way she looked was the way she acted. I had expected her to bounce out like a love-starved kangaroo but instead she just sauntered down the terrace steps, half smiling, and acting like a cat that's spotted a bird with a broken wing and knows it's as good as caught.

It scared me because she was smiling just like she had found out something about me. There wasn't anything to do but smile back like there wasn't anything to find out about me, but when I did I felt myself starting to blush and the harder I tried to stop blushing the more I did blush, so finally I just broke down and asked her what she was smiling about.

"You!" she said and she looked so pleased with herself that she almost started laughing. "You've had it, Deacon. Now why don't you take off that halo and stop acting!"

My smile really turned sickly then because all I could think of was that she had found out about me and Lacey and knew that we had been out by the pool until two o'clock that morning. Then I realized there wasn't any way she could have found out.

I had left Sim Everette's dock in my boat around eight-thirty. I had come down the river, tied up, taken a path up the slope, across River Road, taken the path up through the pines that bordered the Belton estate, slipped into their big formal garden from the back and there was Lacey waiting for me in the moonlight by the pool.

I had stayed until around two oclock and then I'd gone back down to my boat the same way I had come. I'd done it at least fifty times before and not a soul had ever dreamed I was any place but out on the river plugging for bass or running trotlines. Or suspected anything about Lacey either. She just liked to sit out in the garden at night the same way she liked to go out to their lodge on the river by herself.

And last night hadn't been any different from any other night. Pert had come in from her date around eleven o'clock, which was early for her, but we had heard her go in the house. And around midnight Lacey had thought she heard a car in the driveway and had gone up to check but there hadn't been anybody, she said. So Pert couldn't know anything.

So I stood there staring down at her, wondering just what she was talking about but, before I could ask, a door opened and slammed and Lacey came out on the terrace. She had changed from her church clothes into a white linen dress but it was one of those fitted kind and with her golden hair and her proud, beautiful face and her long, slim, tan legs and everything else accented so, she was even more disturbing than Pert. She spotted us as soon as she came out and, seeing how pale I was, she thought that Pert was up to her old tricks.

"All right, Passion Flower!" she snapped. "Exhale!"

She had reference to the way Pert had her shoulders back and her chest out trying to distract me, but Pert just smiled real innocently and said that she wasn't doing a thing, that I was just asking her for a date.

Well, like I've said, Lacey was used to that kind of talk so she just ignored Pert's remark and greeted me as though I was just making a social call on Kip and told me to come on. We headed down the rock walk that led through the formal garden to the pool and I felt like Adam sneaking back into the Garden of Eden. Especially with Pert trailing along behind us. She could have been the cherub with the flaming sword.

She wasn't saying anything, just smiling and humming something that sounded like the Funeral March. That worried me because a talking woman ain't necessarily a thinking woman, but a humming woman, she *is* thinking, and usually she is real pleased with her thoughts, And I couldn't help wondering what them pleasing thoughts were because I hadn't forgot a word she'd said about me taking off my halo and stopping my acting.

But there wasn't a word spoke until we reached the pool. It was set in the middle of the garden and ringed around by lawn and flower beds and spruces and at the near end there was a patio, sort of, with sun couches and lawn chairs and a couple of tables with big, fancy umbrellas sprouting out of the middle. With the sunshine and a soft breeze blowing, it should've been a real pretty spot but one thing spoiled it all ... Kip Belton.

If he was the murderer, he sure wasn't doing any cringing or skulking. He was in his swimming trunks, rared back on a sun couch with a drink in his hand, trying to look like a sultan or something surveying his palace grounds. I felt right sorry for him because I knew he thought I ought to be impressed but he had just picked the wrong piece of furniture. The couch he was stretched out on was the same one that I had loved his wife on until two o'clock that morning.

But when he sat up and glared at us I didn't feel sorry for him any more because he was just about the most arrogant fellow there was and had less excuse for it. He had sweaty, black hair, a flat, beefy face, reddish blue eyes and a knob of a nose that his drinking hadn't helped either. It was laced with such a web of little busted blood vessels that it made you think he had spiders in his system.

And the rest of him even made his head look good. He was naturally big, about six foot two, and at one time he'd had a real good build, but by watching his eating and drinking he had managed to overcome it. He had grown himself one of these box stomachs. A barrel stomach is the normal kind, in that it's rounded off at the sides, but a box stomach is narrow and all out in front of you and that was Kip's. From the back he didn't look fat but when he turned around you could see that he weighed about two hundred and fifty pounds and there wasn't a pretty ounce in the bunch.

But it wasn't his face or his stomach that made him so outstandingly unattractive, it was his air. He measured everybody by their money and he just couldn't be civil to anybody with less than a million dollars. It just seemed to hurt his ears to hear a poor man talk and he would sigh and roll his eyes and fidget like he just couldn't wait for you to get through so he could tell you how stupid you were.

And that's the way he tried acting when he saw us, like he was doing us a favor admitting us into his presence, but he didn't get away with it because he was the one thing that Pert and Lacey had in common. They both loathed him. Lacey loathed him because she was his wife and Pert loathed him because, in a couple of his drunken fits, he had tried making a wife out of her too. At least that's what Lacey had told me and she wouldn't repeat anything that horrible unless it was the positive truth. That was another reason I knew somebody would have to kill him and one reason I felt sorry for Pert.

So she ignored his glaring at us and stared down at his big hairy stomach. "Well," she smirked, "if it isn't King Farouk!"

"Really?" Lacey said. "I thought it was Friar Tuck!"

Now that was like pouring hot grease in his ears but he acted like he hadn't even heard them and looked at me and sighed, "All right, Reverend, what the hell do you want now?" He called me Reverend because he liked to think of himself as a sport and all *Christians* as perverts but I didn't say anything about it, I just told him that what I wanted to talk about was Rita. He gave another big sigh then.

"Reverend, can't you handle anything by yourself? *You're* the Chief of Police. *I'm* a businessman. I've got a three-million-dollar business to run but ..."

That was as far as Pert let him get. "Knock it off, Daddy Warbucks!" she said. "Any idiot with an order blank and a pencil could run that business and you know it and, if you didn't want to be Police Commissioner, why did you beg Mr. Phelps to appoint you?"

"Don't you know?" Lacey said. "So he could blow his little siren and carry that silly pistol. Of course, the only reason Mr. Phelps gave him the job was that nobody else but Stool Williams would take it!"

Well, like I've said, poor Stool was the town half-wit and was crazy about western movies, and every time he'd meet you on the street he'd have to show you how fast he could draw, and go "pow-pow" at you like his fingers were pistols. I'd always stagger and clutch at my stomach like he had shot me but Kip didn't think he was funny at all and, when Lacey said what she did, he bounced to his feet and started shaking his fist at her and Pert.

"You shut your damn mouths, you hear me? Both of you."

I almost felt sorry for him again because every time he shook that fist his stomach jiggled and Pert got to laughing.

"If you can't get a girdle for that thing," she said, "why don't you take it down to the cotton gin and get it baled?"

Lacey started laughing and that was more than he could stand. "You little bitch!" he snarled at Pert and drew back to slap her. And he would've done it except that I grabbed him and slammed him back on the couch and that really made him mad.

"You river-rat sonofabitch," he bellowed, "get out of here!"

I should've hit him but I wanted to put my plan through. "Just tell me one thing," I said. "Did you break up a party at Rita's last night?"

"Hell, yes, I broke it up. Somebody had to. You were out on that damn river as usual."

That's when I should've left but I couldn't because Pert jumped back into things. It was the first she'd heard of him having been anywhere near Rita's.

"Arrest him, Buck!" she giggled. "I'll bet he did it!"

There went my plan.

"Damn you!" he snarled at Pert. "I was in bed at midnight."

"*Whose* bed?" Pert said. "Rita's?"

Just for a second he hesitated, then he turned and glared right at me. "I was in bed with my wife!"

Well, that was such a bare-faced lie I didn't know what to do, but I did know I couldn't just stand there gaping at him. Any second Lacey might start clawing at his eyes and screaming that he was lying and he would know that we were after him.

"All right," I wheezed, "but, if you lay one finger on Pert, so help me God, I'll come back here and ..."

"Get out!" he said.

I turned and started back down the walk and Pert and Lacey jumped up and came with me. Pert laughed and carried on all the way back to the house. I didn't hear a word she said and Lacey didn't seem to either. They walked out to the car with me and I told them good-by and thanked them for their trouble. Pert squeezed my hand and gave me a smile that, I realized later, should have scared me to death. Then she ran up the terrace steps. Lacey watched her and then, real quick, turned to me. "I'll be at the lodge!" Then she turned and went up the steps.

The lodge was on their farm up the river and we spent nights there because she was the only one who used it. I could already hear her questions. Had Kip lost his mind? Why did he say he had been in bed with her at midnight? He'd *never* been in bed with her. Didn't he know that the reason she didn't call him a liar was that she wanted to find out what he was up to?

Those would be her questions and, as I got in my car, I tried thinking of the answers. There just didn't seem to be any. He'd been drinking but even falling-down drunk he ought to know there wasn't any way he could make Lacey back up his alibi. She hated him, she wasn't scared of him, he couldn't bribe her, he couldn't... All of a sudden I could feel my bowels icing up. There *was* a way he could make her alibi for him! Blackmail!

If he had found out about us, if he knew that we had been out in the garden committing adultery the night before he could blackmail us both.

The sweat started puddling up in my shoes and I tried telling myself that I was just being spooked by my own conscience but I couldn't make myself listen. Blackmail was the only thing that made any sense and the only thing he could blackmail her about was me. But that was enough. She could testify that she wasn't in bed with him but to prove it she would have to testify that she wasn't in bed at all, she was out in the garden having relations with Deacon Peters.

And it wouldn't be just plain testifying, it would be testifying in front of a whole courtroom full of people—deacons, elders, Reverend Samuels, the Golden Rule Bible Class, my Sunday School class, all the sweet old ladies in town including her mother and my mother.

If he was the murderer, I didn't have him, *he had me!*

CHAPTER SIX

S O ON MY WAY HOME I tried telling myself that sending Kip Belton to the electric chair would be worth the disgrace it would bring me, but when I sneaked into the house it was like the Devil had overheard me and wanted to show me what a lie it was. I looked out my bedroom window and there was Mama and three of her elderly friends sitting out on the back lawn discussing the case and saying what a blessing it was that I was handling it. They had me sounding like a cross between Sherlock Holmes and John the Baptist because they said I was the only man in town with hands and conscience clean enough to snatch the covers off of. everybody that had ever been at Rita's.

Miss Nellie Heath was leading the discussion. She's a tall, long-faced woman and her bottom eyelids sag so that she has to blink a lot to keep her eyeballs in. That makes her look like a nervous basset hound but she can be right militant.

"Buck Peters is God's own!" she snapped. "He's one boy the Beast ain't bit."

That was what she called sex, "The Beast," and Mrs. Cad Johnson knew just what she meant because she got to shaking worse than ever. She's got palsy and talking about sex aggravates it.

"Amen!" she said. "Buck Peters is more man than any man in this town but you don't find any sheet burns on him. No, sir, that boy's never been bedridden."

With that Miss Hattie Ebersole joined in. "That's just what I tell my nephew. I say, 'Why can't you be like Buck Peters? He don't have to chase girls to have a good time. Why can't you go out on the river with him?' "

Well, Mama just sat there fanning and beaming and I knew right then I couldn't get up in any courtroom and tell the town what Lacey and I had been doing in that garden at midnight. It would just kill Mama and Miss Nellie's eyeballs would fall plumb out and poor old Mrs. Johnson would shake herself to pieces. Besides Miss Hattie's nephew had a mouth the size of a coat sleeve and I could just hear him whooping that he wished he *had* gone out on the river with me. The reason I didn't chase girls, he'd tell Miss Hattie, was that I already had one staked out.

Just the thought of it killed any appetite I might have had for lunch, so I changed into my uniform for my trip up the river and hid Rita's diary in my closet and left a note for Mama saying I might be out on the case all night and then I sneaked out of the house and went back down to the City Hall.

Things were just as bad as I figured they would be. The four loafing benches out front were loaded with all the elderly, dena-tured, woman-proof members of the Sitting and Spitting Society and they were hooting and hollering and drawing names out of a hat that Charlie Rowland was passing around. Charlie was the ringleader of the group and every woman and drunk in town wanted to kill him. If a woman was going to have a baby he would get up a pool on what day the baby would come into the world, and if a drunk was drinking himself to death he would get up a pool on what day he would be leaving this world. There just wasn't anything he wouldn't get up a pool on and this time he had got up a pool on who Rita's murderer was and put the names of half the men in town in the hat. When he saw me drive up he whooped to the customers that Charlie Turner and Sid Crocker and Kip Belton were still in the hat and they better get 'em before it was too late.

I put a stop to that real fast. I told him I hadn't caught the murderer but that if he sold one more chance and couldn't show me a gambling stamp I was throwing him in jail.

He got all hurt and said he never had seen me so touchy before and offered to give me Kip Belton in the pool free if I'd let him keep on peddling the chances. I just ignored him and went on into the station. It wasn't any better in there because Chink Weatherman who relieved Chastain said that Dawd Rankin had left a note for me.

Dawd was the Sheriff and handled things out in the County and he had been elected just because he hated to arrest people, especially registered voters. If you had as many as ten votes in your family, Dawd would let you get away with anything but murder and even then he would try to let the statute of limitations run out on you. Unless, of course, you had murdered somebody who had eleven votes in his family.

And just like I figured, the note said that he would dearly love to help me on the case but unfortunately his poor mother had had another bad stroke and he would have to be at her side for the next week or so. That's the way it always happened. Any time he was afraid that *he* might have to arrest somebody his mother always got a bad stroke. That made the twenty-seventh one she was supposed to have had in the past two years and she still looked healthier than Dawd.

And no sooner did I get the note read than Toad Francis, the editor of the *Greenhill Gazette,* came in. Toad's ears are so big his head looks like a wing nut and he's one of these hell-raising country editors but he's real particular about who he raises it with. It's always with Russians and Chinamen and Mau-Maus and other such people that ain't very likely to run any ads or tax notices in his paper. So he came in all whiteeyed and breathless like he was afraid that the murderer might be one of his big advertisers.

When I told him I hadn't caught the murderer, he gave a big sigh of relief and said that since his paper didn't come out till Thursday he just didn't think that he would mention the case at all because it wouldn't be news by then. I hated to lie about it but I went ahead and agreed with him.

"And I wouldn't bother those city newspapers you correspond for about it," I said. They were the ones I was scared of. Mine and Lacey's love was a sacred thing but they probably wouldn't regard it as such. I could see big black headlines about the "diddling deacon."

"Oh, I'm sure the city papers wouldn't be interested," Toad said. "But I'll tell you what I'll do. I'll hold my back page open and if you catch the murderer between now and Thursday I'll give you a nice, dignified little story on it. Provided, of course, the murderer ain't a local fellow."

Well, I thanked him and he left and I felt some better but not for long because Reverend Samuels called and said that he had just got up off his knees praying for the Lord to help me with the case, also the Men's Bible Class was all ready to be deputized if they could help out.

It was real touching and I got depressed all over again about my sins but I put up a brave front. I thanked him for his prayers and told him what a comfort it was to have the Men's Bible Class behind me and that I would sure call on them, if the occasion arose. He said, fine, that we Christians had to close ranks and then he hung up, leaving me feeling like Judas with the eleven other disciples closing ranks on him.

Then my troubles really commenced: Delbert and Weenie Thomas, the cab driver, came through the door. They were both snapping and snarling at one another and I couldn't help groaning.

Weenie was a tall, blond, skinny boy about my age and had eyes set so close together he looked like a flounder but I liked him, despite him having the same sort of anemia of the soul that Delbert did, and, because of some favors I had done him, he was very devoted to me too. As for him and Delbert snapping at one another, that was their custom. They couldn't agree on Delbert's standing in the community. Delbert claimed that he was a guardian of the people but Weenie claimed that he wasn't nothing but a servant of the people and why the hell didn't he act like one.

He sure wasn't acting like one this time. He slammed the door shut and leveled his finger at Weenie and snarled, "This silly sonofabitch has busted the case wide open. He took the murderer out to Rita's last night and *left* him on her doorstep."

Well, from the way he said it and the way Weenie was glaring at him, I couldn't tell whether he was kidding or not. He said he wasn't.

"The brainless bastard," he said, glaring back at Weenie, "was out at the VFW club last night. It was his night off from driving the cab but around midnight his partner, Tooley Burns, who had the cab, got a sudden attack of the crud or something. Well, not knowing how disgustingly drunk Weenie had got himself, he called up the club and told the bartender to tell Weenie to pick up the cab at the stand and take over.

"Well, being how Weenie is one of those maniacs who thinks he can drive better when he's drunk, he picked up the cab and *another* jug of Old Stomach Pump and at some place, at some time after midnight, *some* man got him to take him out to Rita's and leave him. At least he thinks he left him. He ain't sure. Maybe he left Weenie. It's the damnedest thing I ever heard of."

And with that he glared at Weenie even harder and Weenie glared right back and asked him if he always called taxpayers "silly sonsofbitches." I started getting exasperated because it was beginning to look like Kip wasn't our man after all and I couldn't tell whether I was sorry or not.

Delbert could see I was getting mad so he told Weenie to go ahead and tell me what had happened, that he didn't have the heart himself. So Weenie started in. He said that he did get to drinking somewhat after he picked the cab up and after midnight things did get kind of confusing.

"But there's one thing I remember, Buck," he said. "I remember going out River Road and seeing this man walking along. Then I picked him up and took him out to Rita's and left him. That much I do remember."

I could tell by the disgusted look on Delbert's face that there was more to it than that so I asked Weenie just how come, when everything else was so drunk and confusing, he remembered picking the man up.

"Because," he said, "some things stick in your mind no matter how drunk you are. I didn't see this fellow walking alongside the road. I nearly ran over him and when I backed up to tell him I was sorry, I nearly ran over him again."

I couldn't help joining Delbert in a sigh.

"You remember all that," I said, "but you don't remember his face?"

"I never saw his face," he said. "When I backed up to apologize, I didn't see anybody at first and then, all of a sudden, I heard some cussing and there was this fellow dodging around in the road. I jammed on my brakes and, the next thing I knew, he was getting in the back of my cab. He must have dove into the ditch the first time I nearly hit him, and then when he came back up on the road and saw me weaving back toward him again, he must have headed for the other ditch and I must have caught him halfway across the road, so ..."

"So," Delbert snorted, "he must have decided, if he couldn't beat you, he'd better join you, so the poor bastard piled in. Of course, you didn't recognize his voice?"

"No, you sonofabitch, I didn't. I heard him scream when I nearly *ran* over him and I heard him scream when I nearly *backed* over him but I never heard him talk in no normal voice."

"Then just how the hell did you know to take him out to Rita's?" Delbert said. "I guess he screamed that too?"

"I don't know," Weenie said. "Maybe I was going out there too."

"*You* were going out there?" Delbert said. "It's a good thing I didn't *catch* you going out there!"

What he meant was that Rita had drove Weenie crazier than anybody and he just wouldn't leave her alone and finally he pestered her so much that she had taken out a warrant to make him stay away from her.

"Delbert," I sighed, "that's all beside the point. Weenie was drunk."

"Of course, I was drunk," Weenie said, "and if I *was* going out there, I was probably just going by to see if she had pulled her shades down like she don't do half the time. But all I remember for sure was turning down the road to Rita's and side-swiping a tree alongside the road and the sonofabitch, whoever he was, hopping out and turning down her driveway. And, if he hadn't wanted to go to Rita's, why did he do that? Why didn't he go back up to the main road?"

"You sure it was Rita's driveway?" I said.

"I'm positive. For one thing there ain't any other driveway on that road and for another thing I went back out there a while ago and there was this chrome-plated tree alongside the road all skinned up, so I know it was the one I side-swiped. And, like I say, he jumped out when I hit the tree and I know he went down Rita's driveway because he hadn't paid me and I started to go down the driveway after him. But when I backed off from the tree and tried going down the driveway, I didn't make the turn and went in the ditch. So I just hollered down and told him that he was a damn poor sport jumping out that way. He never even turned. He just headed straight toward the house."

"But do you remember seeing him knock on the door or go around back or anything?" I said. "You didn't hear any shots?"

"All I remember was taking another big drink to give me the strength to wrestle my cab out of the ditch and the next thing I remember it was around seven o'clock and I was at Mary's café and she was pouring coffee down me and Tooley was there wanting to know just what the hell I had been doing with the cab, playing polo? Then I went home and woke up around two o'clock and went back to Mary's and had some breakfast and everybody was talking about the murder. Well, I didn't say anything because I wanted to make sure first that what I'd been through wasn't just a nightmare or something. So I went out to Rita's to check and there was the skinned-up tree and this smart aleck Delbert was snooping around for clues as he called it. Well, I wanted to help *you* out, Buck, so I told him what I knew and I ain't heard a civil word out of the sonofabitch since. He's got the poorest manners of any policeman I ever saw."

Delbert wanted to bandy words with him about that but I shut him up and asked Weenie if he got any idea about the man's size.

"He was big!" he said. "That's the reason I didn't go down Rita's driveway after him on foot. He was so big I must've figured it'd be safer to run over him with my cab than hit him with my fist."

"Was he drunk, you think?"

"He got in that cab with me, didn't he? He had to be drunk or crazy one. Besides, what man in his right mind would take a cab to commit a murder?"

"Well, now, Weenie," I said, "even though you didn't get a good look at this fellow's face, did you, at any time, have the feeling that you might know him. Like you could sense who it was?"

"Yeah!" he said.

"Who?" I said.

He sighed. "Well, now maybe this is just hoping on my part because the fellow I thought he was is the fellow I'd rather send to the chair than anybody!"

Delbert's face lit all up at that. "Kip Belton?"

"Yeah," Weenie sighed.

He had a right to sigh. He had had a real pretty sister at one time and Kip had gone after her. She was a fairly nice girl but Kip was so intent on getting her that he gave her all sorts of expensive presents and pretty soon she convinced herself that he really was in love with her and wanted to marry her—despite everybody telling her that he wasn't after but one thing. Well, after about four months, when Kip had evidently got what he was after, he dropped her and she committed suicide. The gossips all said it was because she was pregnant and Kip still wouldn't marry her.

Anyway, it was real tragic and for that reason I wouldn't let myself put too much faith in Weenie's hunch about it being Kip in his cab.

"Weenie," I said, "you despise the very sight of Kip Belton so don't you think you would have realized, for sure, it was him, no matter how drunk you were? And don't you think that, after you had the feeling it was him, you would've at least made him get out?"

"I guess so," he said, "but I was awful drunk and I didn't get the feeling it was him until I saw him going down the driveway. But then I figured that it must not be him because this fellow had been walking and that bastard Belton ain't walked a foot since he was old enough to get a driver's license. But that's the only thing. This fellow was big enough and drunk enough."

"Yeah!" said Delbert who was all on Weenie's side now. "And if he was drunk enough to get in that cab with you, he could have been so drunk that he'd run his car off the road some place and couldn't get out to Rita's any way except by walking. And maybe that's the reason you nearly hit him. He was drunk and weaving alongside the road."

Weenie cut his eyes at me. "Now you can accuse me of hind-sighting, if you want to, but it seems to me that I did pass a car half in the ditch alongside River Road some place because I remember snarling to myself that they ought to keep drunks off the road."

Well, I looked at Delbert and Delbert looked at me and Weenie started waking up.

"You mean, you think it really might be him?" he said. "You got something else on him?"

"Hell, yes, we have!" Delbert said, and started telling him everything. I let him go ahead. For one thing, I knew that Weenie could be trusted to keep his mouth shut, especially if it meant sending Kip to the chair. But the main thing was that I was beginning to think that maybe I could wiggle out of the trap Kip had me in. *If* we could somehow prove that Kip had been in Weenie's cab, then *Weenie* could bust Kip's alibi about having been in bed with Lacey at midnight. I wouldn't have to say a word about being in the garden.

But there was still the problem of proving that he had actually done the shooting. Rita could have been dead when he got there and he could be lying the way he was just because he didn't want to get mixed up in the case.

"Now, Weenie," I said, "it sounds like you've put us on to something real good but don't get your hopes too high. Kip's our chief suspect but we got others."

And with that I asked Delbert what he'd found out about Dr. Winston and Clyde Mansfield and the rest. He sighed and said that he'd talked to one of the orderlies at the hospital and, in a roundabout way, he'd found out that Dr. Winston had got to the hospital around two o'clock to deliver that baby, but the baby wasn't ready and he'd gone out to get something to eat, but he hadn't got back until around four o'clock, about twenty minutes before the baby came.

"That's just what I said could've happened," I told Weenie. "He could've done it."

Well, Weenie wanted to know why Dr. Winston would have wanted to kill Rita but Delbert told him never mind, and then he said that he'd found out that Phil and Sam hadn't taken Clyde Mansfield home, they dropped him off at Hook Phillips's joint and he'd left there around three o'clock.

"But that don't mean anything," he said. "Sam and Phil had to take so many of those drunks home that they probably forgot about dropping Clyde off at Hook's and he probably just went on home after he left there. But what *does* mean something is that I talked to all of Kip's cronies and girls, just the way you said talk to 'em, Buck, and not a one of 'em mentioned seeing him all night so he must have been by himself after midnight and it ain't hard to imagine what he was doing."

Well, that wound up his report and brought us to the point I had been dreading. He wanted to hear *my* report. "What did *you* find out?" he said. "You been talking to the bastard in person, but with that stupid plan you got I don't guess you let him open his lying mouth!"

There wasn't anything to do but tell him the truth. I told him how Kip had got mad and Pert had stampeded him into blurting out an alibi. "He claims," I said, "that at midnight he was in bed with Lacey."

Weenie looked real disappointed but Delbert just looked disgusted. "And I guess Lacey backed him up. That's the reason you're just now telling us."

"I couldn't ask her," I said, "without arousing his suspicions."

"Yes, you could!" he said. "You just didn't want to because you knew what she'd say. No matter how much a woman hates her husband, she'll lie to save him from the chair and you know it!"

I kept on crawfishing. "I don't know any such thing," I said. "She'll probably say that she don't know whether he was in bed at midnight or not. She'll probably say that she was asleep at midnight."

Now that was just what I was going to have her say or pretty close to it. Just have her say that she didn't know *where* he was at midnight. It wouldn't be an out-and-out lie and it would save her good name and it wouldn't help Kip.

"Besides," I went on, "if we can *prove* that Kip was in Weenie's cab, it won't make any difference what she says. She won't have to say anything."

"I'm gonna call her!" Delbert said.

I got real brave then. "Go ahead," I said. "I'll talk to her!"

He smiled real nasty, like he didn't believe it, and dialed the number. Then he asked for her. Then his smile faded and he put the phone down. "The butler says she's gone out to their lodge on the river and won't be back until tomorrow morning."

"That'll be plenty of time," I said. "It'll give you and Weenie time to check over his cab and see if you can find anything, or check over the route he took, things like that."

"Sure!" he said. "Of course, you couldn't run out to that lodge and ask her now."

"I might," I said. "I'm going up the river to ask some of the shanty-boaters if they saw anybody tie up at dock at the foot of Rita's road. Then maybe I'll just keep on up river to the Beltons' lodge and ask her."

"I'll bet!" he sneered.

And with that I headed for Sim Everette's dock and my boat and Lacey.

CHAPTER SEVEN

WELL, by five o'clock I had picked up my boat at Sim's dock and was roaring along upriver about a mile above town. The evening breeze was rippling the water and what with the sun hitting it from straight ahead the whole river was glittering like a big, green, diamond-studded snake. The valley itself had a sort of warm, golden green glow to it and it was all so peaceful and pretty that I almost forgot my troubles. Then a flash of light off in the distance, way up the hill above River Road, caught my eye. It was the sun hitting the windows of the Belton mansion. It looked like a big white castle set amongst doll houses and the sight of it opened up the seams of my soul and got me to thinking about Lacey again.

After that day on the river, when we were sixteen and she had made a slave of love out of me, we officially became sweethearts and all the parents in town thought we were just the finest young Christian couple that ever was and kept wishing that their sons and daughters would be more like us. I just thanked the Lord that they weren't. Not that we weren't Christians. We were, all except for one thing. Every Sunday afternoon we would take a canoe trip up to that pretty little clearing along the river where I had first become enslaved and I would come back so exhausted that I would hardly have the strength to preside at the Young People's Christian Union meeting that night.

That went on for two years and when I graduated from high school I got a football scholarship to State. It wasn't exactly a regular conference scholarship-free books, laundry, and fifteen dollars a month—it was one of those alumni type scholarships and was a little better. In fact, they gave me $12,000 a year plus a new car every year.

I felt right bad about that so every year I would give Mama all the money except for two thousand dollars. I would take that and give it to Lacey's Uncle Martin Satterfield so they could send her to college. They didn't have money enough to do it themselves and I asked only two things in return. One was that nobody was to know where the money came from, and the other was that Lacey was to be free to choose her own school.

Well, with all the schools in this country she had to choose from, she chose the one I was going to. And, in view of the agreement I had made with her Uncle Martin, there wasn't any way I could stop her, so for four years she had me living up to my lover's oath. If it hadn't been for that I think I would have made All-American my sophomore year too.

It was sinful all right but there wasn't any way out for me and besides I kept trying to make her marry me. Every time I'd mention it, though, she would just laugh and say that she *was* going to marry me but she had to marry Kip Belton first. I thought she was saying that just to be coy or aggravating or something because Kip was going to State too and, although he had the longest car and more money than anybody in school and was always trying to get Lacey to go with him, she treated him like a dirty little boy.

Well, the spring of my senior year I finally persuaded the Marines that my trick knee wasn't as bad as the doctors said so they took me and sent me off to Korea. I did win some medals but I was scared the whole time and them heathen Chinamen with them bugles made a whole lot better Christian out of me than Reverend Samuels had. When I wasn't fighting I was praying or writing Lacey to stop sending me such passionate letters because I was a reformed man and I was going into missionary work, if I ever got out of that mess alive.

And I really meant to do it but, when I got back to San Francisco, there she was waving at me from the dock and looking more beautiful than ever. She said that she and her Uncle Martin had come out on a vacation and were going to drive me home to Green-hill. Not only that but they had a hotel room reserved for me and everything.

Well, I was mighty grateful and went to the hotel with her but when we got up to the room Uncle Martin wasn't there and Lacey said she guessed he had gone out to see the seals or Alcatraz or something. Well, as soon as she said that I headed for the door, but before I was halfway there she had me around the neck kissing me and I was trying to break loose, all the time reminding her of my missionary oath.

It just didn't work, though. About the third time she kissed me I realized that if there was one thing that a missionary wasn't, it was ungrateful, so I told her that in view of all that she and Uncle Martin had done for me, I would fulfill my lover's oath to her one more time but that would be all.

Well, about two hours later, when I was still fulfilling my oath, there was, all of a sudden, this knocking at the door. It just plain nearly scared me to death because I didn't have a thing on but a sheet and neither did Lacey and I knew that it must be either Uncle Martin or the house detective at the door. All I could think of was snatching on some clothes and jumping out the window, even if it was twelve floors up. Suicide before shame, I thought, but before I could make a move Lacey had locked her arms around my neck and was whispering that if I didn't lie still she was going to scream.

There wasn't anything I *could* do but lie still because any time a boy jumps out of a hotel window with a naked girl wrapped around his neck there's bound to be talk. So the knocking got worse and Lacey got weirder. I wheezed to her that she had lost her mind, that we had better do something because it was Uncle Martin or the house detective at the door but she just ignored me and said that if I didn't renew my vows to always be her lover, no matter what, she would *really* scream.

There went my missionary career. I renewed all the vows I'd ever made her and with that she gave me the nastiest shock a man ever got, especially a man in my particular position. She untwined her arms from around my neck, grinned up at me, and whispered, "That's Kip at the door. We were married last week. We're on our honeymoon!"

I just gaped at her for about twenty seconds and finally I gasped that she was lying. She grinned bigger than ever and said no, she wasn't. She'd left a note for him at the desk telling him to come up to this room, that an old friend wanted to see him.

Kip finally stopped knocking and went away and she started explaining. She said she had owed it to her father's memory to marry Kip and if she hadn't married him before I got back she never would have. Then she stopped grinning and said there was one thing I would have to believe: She had told him before they got married that she didn't love him and never would be anything but a wife-in-name-only to him and was marrying him just for his money and to drive him crazy.

He hadn't believed her but she had shown him. He had tried making love to her on their honeymoon night and she had laughed in his face and had kept on laughing even when he tried to strangle her. He knew now that she had meant what she said and that his only hope was wearing her down. But he never would, she said. After she got even with him for everything the Beltons had done to the Satterfields, she was coming to me untouched by any hands but mine, a fit wife for any missionary.

Now maybe I ought've flown into a holy rage at her, because it looked like she loved revenge more than she did me and, besides that, in just a matter of seconds she had turned me from a plain fornicator into the fanciest sort of adulterator, but I loved her too much and understood her too well to be anything but sorry for her.

Her daddy and Kip's daddy had been in the timber business. Kip's daddy had pulled off a deal that was to make the business one of the biggest in the South but it was one of them deals that technically wasn't crooked but morally it was and rather than go along with it, Lacey's daddy dissolved the partnership. Then he sold his big, beautiful home and about everything else he had to pay off the people that Kip's daddy had swindled in his name.

The worry and the strain broke him body and soul. He had a stroke and spent his last two years as an invalid. I could remember, as a boy, passing the boarding house that Lacey's mama was running to support them and seeing him sitting on the front porch with a blanket over his lap, staring out into space. Lacey was only in the fourth grade or so then but she would be sitting at his side trying to read to him and act as his nurse.

And I could remember even better than that the licking I'd give Kip Belton and a friend of his when they stopped in front of the boarding house one afternoon and started making fun of him because he couldn't talk or move.

Then, when he was dying, Lacey slipped into his room. He couldn't hug her or tell her anything, all he could do was try to smile at her with his eyes, she said. She started crying and swore to him that she was going to get even with the Beltons for everything they had done to him and she was going to make Kip Belton sorry he had ever been born.

And those were the thoughts I was thinking, starting up the river that afternoon. They took the sparkle off the water and put a chill in the air but there was one comfort. Lacey had done to the Beltons just about what she told me she was going to do that afternoon in the hotel room.

By goading Kip into doing some drunken bragging about all his money, she had learned enough to ruin him with just one trip to the Internal Revenue boys. Instead of taking that trip, though, she had spent his money any way she wanted to and dared him to stop her. She had bought the Satterfield mansion back and settled her mama and her Uncle Martin in it and with her cold, frosty ways she had managed to make pompous old Mrs. Belton, Sr., feel so much like a field hand that she spent all of her time traveling.

But as comforting as all that was it didn't change the fact that the Belton-Satterfield feud had now reached a stand-off. Lacey had Kip by the throat but he had her too and I was caught right between 'em. We could bust his alibi and send him to the electric chair but the shock he would get wouldn't be much worse than the shock people in town would get when he told them about me and Lacey in the garden. His ordeal would be over in a matter of seconds but mine and Lacey's would go on the rest of our lives.

The Belton lodge was about ten miles upriver from town and, with a motor as big as I had, I could've made the run in about forty minutes easy but I didn't want to get there before dark so I stopped along the way and chatted with some of the shanty-boaters and commercial fishermen about the murder. They said the only man from town they'd noticed on the river the night before was Mr. Phelps and that wasn't anything unusual because he was the biggest fool about fishing they'd ever seen. Well, for his kind of fishing, he *was* the biggest fool I'd ever seen too but I didn't suspect him either because his own lodge, his Temple of Aphrodite as he called it, was just about five miles upriver from the Belton lodge and he had probably been up to it.

So with all that talk I wound up at eight o'clock, good dark, just off the mouth of Hurricane Creek. The lodge sat on the bluff just above the junction of the creek and the river and I could see that Lacey had the light burning in the big downstairs bedroom so I knew everything was all right. I turned into the creek, eased my boat into the boat house, got out and started up the steps to the lodge.

Kip's daddy had built the lodge and despite it looking real rustic from the outside, it was fancied up on the inside something sinful. And sin was just what he'd had in mind. He had practically made a girls' dormitory out of it he had brought so many of 'em out for the night. But when he had died, Kip and Pert and their mother just let it sit because they didn't want any part of the country. Then, when Kip had married Lacey, she had taken it over and every time she would get extra mad at him she would come out. And being as vain as he was, he didn't have any idea that she used it for anything but sulking.

Well, usually when I would start up the steps from the boat house I would take them four at the time but not this evening because I figured that Lacey would be all upset about Kip finding out about us and I would have to cheer her up by telling her a lot of lies about how things weren't as bad as she thought.

So I just eased up the steps and when I got to the top I sneaked up to the kitchen window and peeked in. I had thought she might be on her knees in prayer or reading the Twenty-Third Psalm or something comforting like that, but instead she had this little radio on and it was playing something catchy and she was sitting on a stool humming and singing along with the music and dicing slices of chicken into a salad bowl.

That just made me feel worse. For one thing she looked so beautiful sitting there. All the coldness she had shown at church and all the hardness she had shown when I questioned Kip was gone. She was barefooted and had on white shorts and a white, short-sleeved shirt waist and her shiny gold hair done up in a pony tail and, what with being so tan and healthy and looking so clean and pure, she was the picture of what every man hopes his daughter will grow up to look like. You just never would've dreamed, to look at her, that she was in the mess that she was.

That was something else that made me feel so bad: She was being so brave about everything. She just *couldn't* feel like humming and singing. It was just a brave front she was putting on and she was rehearsing it for me.

At least that's what I thought at the time. I tapped on the door so as not to scare her and then I stepped into the kitchen. Before I could say anything consoling she bounced up off the stool and threw her arms around my neck and started kissing me. It wasn't one of those desperate, thin-lip, panicky kisses like the circumstances warranted. It was one of those soft, warm kisses that makes your eyes dilate and your head feel like it's melting.

I thought that was part of the act she was putting on too, but when I tried to get loose she clamped down on my lower lip with her teeth. That meant she wanted me to keep on kissing her. Most of the time I was glad for her to do that, even though it did leave my lip looking like a teething ring, but this time it just made me feel like something a cannibal had got hold of and I blubbered for her to stop it, that we didn't have time for such foolishness, that we had things to discuss.

She let my lip go and smiled up at me real innocently and said, "What things, Sherlock?"

That's when I really started getting uneasy. I was pretty sure that she was joking, I was pretty sure that she knew that Kip knew about us but she seemed too happy about it all. Maybe she was in shock.

"*What things?*" I said, trying to jar the smile off her face. "Don't you realize that Kip knows about us? He knows that we were in the garden last night. That's the reason he says he was in bed with you. He knows that for us to prove he wasn't we'll have to testify before the whole town that we were out there in the moonlight busting about every commandment there is. Me, a deacon, and you a married woman and a primary department Sunday School teacher."

She didn't smile any more then. Instead she started laughing. "So *that's* why you look so sick?"

"You're the one who's sick!" I said. "We haven't got him, *he's* got *us.*"

She got serious. "Buck, Kip doesn't suspect a thing," she said. "Right after you left at noon he came up to my room and looked even sicker than you do. But mean sick. He said that he had guessed right about me, that I would do anything for his money, wouldn't I? Otherwise I would have wrecked his alibi right in front of you. He'd known I wouldn't. I was just waiting to be bought, wasn't I? All right, if I would back up his alibi he would give me *a divorce and a cash settlement of one million dollars.*"

I stared at her. She was telling the truth but it was still hard to believe. For one thing, Kip knew that Lacey had made an idiot of him with their marriage but he had sworn to show her that he could stick it out longer than she could. For another thing, he was rich but to raise a million dollars cash he would have to sell part of his business.

"Lacey," I said, "did he admit murdering Rita?" He'd practically admitted it with his offer but technically it still wasn't an out-and-out confession.

"He wouldn't admit anything!" she said. "He wouldn't talk about it. In fact, he acted like he wasn't *positive* that he had murdered her but that he was afraid to take any chances trying to prove he hadn't."

She started grinning again. "Buck, here's what I think happened. I think he was so drunk that he couldn't remember anything but the pistol going off and that probably sobered him up. Then, realizing how drunk he had been, he was afraid that, after leaving Rita's the first time, he had blundered somewhere along the line and had left a trail that would eventually lead to him. So not being able to remember where he had been he figured the safest thing to do would be to bribe me into saying that he had been at home. With people knowing how I must feel about him they wouldn't think I would lie to protect him and my testimony would stand up against that of anybody else who might claim to have seen him after midnight."

She took my face in her hands, kissed me on the nose and laughed some more. "We've got him!"

I was too relieved to say anything. Her theory made sense. We did have him. All my fretting had been for nothing. Mama and Miss Lucy and Miss Nellie and Miss Hattie's big mouth nephew and them would not find out about us after all. I started to get down on my knees and thank the Lord but I never made it. Before I could even get Lacey's arms from around my neck she was gloating again.

"Buck, here's the real beauty of it, though. I *acted* like I was going to accept his offer. I told him I was coming out here to sleep on it and would call him tomorrow. And I'm going to tell him that I *will* accept it. Can't you see his face in court when I get up and say, no, he wasn't in bed with me, that he never had been in bed with me, that I wasn't even in bed, *I was out in the garden with you!*"

With that she started hugging me around the neck again and laughing like it was the happiest day of her life. But as hard as she was hugging she couldn't keep the blood from draining out of my face. I was getting sick again. *She wanted the town to know about us.*

Then I remembered Weenie.

"Lacey, listen to me!" I wheezed. "You don't have to tell anybody *anything!*"

Then I told her about Weenie and his drunken driving and taking the drunk out to Rita's. "You don't have to break Kip's alibi!" I said. "All we've got to do is prove that it was Kip in that cab and *Weenie* can break his alibi. We don't have to say a thing. You can save your good name!"

When I said that—about saving her good name—she blinked at me and everything seemed to change. Her smile faded, her joy about having Kip in her clutches seemed to drain away and tears started welling up in her eyes.

"I haven't a good name to save, Buck," she said real softly. "I ruined my name when I married Kip Belton. The only way I can clear it is by bringing this all out in the open, telling everybody that I've never stopped loving you, that I've never been a wife to Kip and that the only reason I married him was because of my father!"

As scared as I was, tears almost started welling up in my eyes too because it was the first time she had ever admitted that she cared what people thought about her marrying Kip. She wasn't near as hard as she acted. Her life with Kip had been even more of a hell than she had admitted. But as sorry as I felt for her I couldn't go encouraging her. I had to think of Mama and all them.

"Lacey," I wheezed, "you've got a good name. You've got the best name of any girl in town!"

She ignored that. She said that everybody knew what the Beltons had done to her daddy and that they would understand. They wouldn't have to know what we were actually doing in the garden. Knowing us they would think that we were just talking.

"I'll tell them that you were just consoling me. And you were too."

I told her that the people in town might think at first I was consoling her but Kip's lawyer wouldn't stop until he had brought out just *how* I was consoling her. Then he would find out about *all* the nights in the garden and *all* the days on the river bank and before it was all over he would be trying to make it look like *we* had killed Rita just to frame Kip.

"The only thing for you to do," I said, "is to say that you were asleep and don't know where Kip was at midnight. Don't mention us. Then let Weenie bust his alibi."

She knew I was making sense and she started getting mad. She said everybody would know better than to believe the lawyer. "They know that the only thing we're guilty of is loving one another and hating Kip. They certainly won't blame us for that."

"They won't blame us for loving one another," I sighed, "but they'll blame us for acting like the Bobbsey twins all these years and making fools out of them. The only thing to do is to leave it all to Weenie!"

She really started getting mad then. She wasn't leaving anything to Weenie, she said. She had waited ever since she was twelve years old to get even with Kip Belton and now that she had him she wasn't going to step aside for any drunken cab driver. She wanted to see the look on Kip's nasty fat face when she told him she had been in the garden with me. She wanted to see the look on his face when she told everybody that she never had been in bed with him.

"How would you like it, if everybody in town thought *you* were sleeping with Kip Belton?"

She was just about shouting and I tried calming her down and telling her that people wouldn't think about her not sleeping with Kip Belton, all they would think about was her sleeping with me. Me, a deacon and the Chief of Police and her, a wife and a Sunday School teacher.

She really started shouting then.

"I'm not any wife, I'm a mistress and you're not any deacon, you're a sex maniac, so what do we care what they think?"

Well, that got me mad and *I* started shouting.

"I may be a sex maniac to you but I'm a deacon to my mama and everybody else and, if you get up on that witness stand, you'll get mad at that lawyer and start telling a bunch of wild tales about us and you'll wipe out every poor old lady in town. There'll be so many heart attacks, Oscar Wright will be three days hauling the bodies over to his funeral home and your own dear mother will be amongst 'em. They're the ones I'm thinking about, not me."

"Buck Peters, that is a lie! You aren't thinking about those old ladies, you're thinking about yourself. You're just like all men. You can make yourself believe anything you want to. Only you're worse. You're the only man in the world who's been committing adultery twelve years and blaming it on God and motherhood. You don't really like it, you just do it because you took a sacred oath to do it to protect your poor mama! Hah!"

I guess it was the outraged look on my face that got her to laughing. Anyway she started in and said that she didn't care what happened, she was going to get up in court and tell everything and she wasn't going to lay the blame just on Kip, she was going to lay it on me too. She said that she couldn't have helped hating Kip, but she could have helped loving me.

"But, no, you *made* me love you. *You raped me.*"

Well, I was so mad that I didn't realize what she was up to. She had made up her mind to expose Kip. She knew it was going to be bad for both of us but it couldn't be helped, so she was trying to cheer me up by kidding me. I was too mad to realize it though.

"Raped you!" I said. "You *raped* me and I never would have touched you again if you hadn't threatened to have me lynched. As for a *man* being able to make *himself* believe anything he wants to, what about…"

I kept on raving and she kept on laughing and I got so carried away defending myself that I didn't notice everything she was doing. The first thing I knew she didn't have but one of her hands around my neck. The other one was unbuckling my belt. I looked down and she had stepped out of her shorts and pants.

But I didn't try to stop her. I just got madder. I was going to show her that I wasn't any sex maniac. I was a Christian and I wasn't going to be swayed by her evil charms any more. So I kept talking and she kept grinning and messing with me. My pants fell down around my ankles and then my shorts and I stepped out of 'em without missing a word. I wanted it to be a real show down.

She just grinned all the more and then she put her arms around the small of my back and drew herself to me and we were just like we had been that first day on the river bank. Only this time there wasn't any screaming. She just tilted her face up to mine and smiled.

"Go on talking!" she said. "I'm listening!"

I tried to. I tried telling her how I was about on the verge of bringing law and order to Greenhill but if she told everybody about us I wouldn't be able to because wouldn't anybody have any respect for me any more. Now that's what I tried telling her. And I did get about halfway through it, but then she started swaying to some music on the radio. Well, my sentences started getting shorter and shorter and then my words started getting farther apart and then I developed a wheeze and finally I couldn't stand it any longer. I grabbed her up in my arms and headed for the bedroom.

Well, she woke me around four the next morning when the alarm went off and about a half an hour later we got up and took a shower. My eyes were so glassy from lack of sleep they looked like they had been shellacked and I felt like I had spent the night with a rodeo, but Lacey was full of talk and when we came out of the shower she looked prettier than ever.

"I had a dream about us last night, Sherlock," she smiled, tossing me a towel to dry her with. "I dreamed that I got up at the trial and told the whole town about us, but instead of becoming a fugitive you became a celebrity and wound up on Ed Sullivan's show and then you made a million dollars endorsing Spring Maid sheets, and I pulled the switch at Kip's electrocution and then we went on a lecture tour for the Kinsey Institute and lived happily ever after. Now wasn't that a nice dream?"

I didn't say anything, I just scrubbed her harder with the towel. She laughed and told me to stop acting like I was waxing a car and quit worrying and go on in and arrest Kip. But not before eight o'clock. At eight she was driving over to the General Store and calling him and telling him that she accepted his offer of the divorce and the million dollars. That would make him stick to that alibi instead of switching to any other one that he might have thought up during the night.

"That wouldn't do at all, would it?" she grinned. "I'll bet you wind up on 'This Is Your Life' too. You can be to sex what Lillian Roth was to whisky. Now dry my front."

She thought she was real funny. I still thought I had a fighting chance of stopping her though. If Delbert and Weenie had found definite proof that Kip had been in the cab, I could confront him with the proof and he wouldn't bother to use Lacey at trial. If she wanted to tell the whole town about us then she'd have to take an ad in the paper.

I finally got her dressed and we went in and had breakfast. Then just before daylight I left the lodge and headed for town. Two miles down river I sheared a pin on my motor and not having another one I had to substitute a nail and nurse my boat in at quarter speed. I didn't tie up at Sim's dock until nine o'clock.

That was bad enough but when I started into Sim's café to call Delbert to come get me I heard this siren whine and he drove up. I knew something was *really* wrong then. I hadn't ever seen him look so disgusted. He stuck his head out the window and snarled, "Where the hell you been?"

I headed for him, telling him a compulsory lie en route. I said my motor had quit on me upriver and I had had to spend the night with a shanty-boater.

"Why?" I said, opening the car door and getting in. "Anything happen?"

He didn't make a move to start the car. Just sat there glaring at me.

"Oh, hell, no, ain't anything happened!" he said. "Nothing except that our star witness, Weenie, has had a wreck and ain't expected to live and Sam and Phil and Kip claim they've caught the murderer. Outside of that, ain't a thing happened!"

CHAPTER EIGHT

GOT in the car and glared right back at Delbert and switched off the ignition. I didn't want him driving, I wanted him talking. I just couldn't believe all that had happened just since I had been gone. I hadn't left until five o'clock Sunday afternoon and it wasn't but nine o'clock Monday morning now.

"Delbert," I said, "I had a hard night on that shanty-boat and I ain't in the mood for jokes."

He sneered that he wasn't joking, that Weenie, with his wild driving, had tried beating Elmer Bell and his lumber truck through an intersection. It had taken them a half an hour to sort Weenie out of the lumber and he was so full of slivers they had a hard time deciding whether to send him to the hospital or the saw mill.

"He's got a three-by-six for a spine," he said, "and if the stupid bastard dies, we won't have to dig him a grave, we can just *drive* him into the ground."

I realized he wasn't joking then. Weenie, he said, was in the hospital under the care of our devoted friend, Dr. Winston, who was going to call us just as soon as he came to, if he ever did.

"As for the murderer," Delbert went on, "Kip and Sam and Phil have made a deal with Stool Williams and that hollow-headed bastard is sitting in a cell like a damn parrot in a cage squawking that he done it."

Well, that almost made me sorry that I was such a good Christian. Stool Williams *was* the village idiot, he *was* a petty thief, a peeping-tom and a couple of equally half-witted women *had* even claimed he had tried to attack them, but he never would murder anybody. *However,* if I let him go ahead and *be* the murderer, it would solve all my problems and wouldn't create any new ones for him which was probably what Kip and Sam and them were thinking in regard to themselves.

The jury would just send him back to the asylum, which he liked because they let him play the jug in the asylum band, and Kip wouldn't have to stand trial and Lacey wouldn't get to deliver her Kinsey Report.

"Now here's the way I figure it happened," Delbert said. "I figure that Sam and Phil, after they left us yesterday, must have got to talking things over and decided that by telling you about Kip, they had slopped the wrong hog. You being so godly, you probably wouldn't have told their wives about them and Rita no matter what happened, but Kip being so ungodly, he would. He would get up at his trial and testify like a vacuum cleaner. He would suck every husband in town into his story about Rita and see how many he could take to his grave with him.

"So then, I figure, they went to Kip and told him that we had conned them into putting the finger on him. They didn't really believe he was the murderer at all though, he was just an innocent, high-spirited boy who liked to josh about shooting girls, if they wouldn't go to bed. The real murderer, they figured, was that crafty, diabolical fiend, Stool Williams, the town nut.

"Well, that probably went over with Kip like an eel in a punch bowl, but at the same time it panicked him because it was the first he knew about our chief suspect. So he probably said they were right on all counts, and they rushed down to Stool's shack and got him all drunked up and made their deal. They probably offered him a couple hundred bucks and a guarantee that Kip's lawyer, Rupe Hobson, could get him off with nothing worse than a couple of years at that Funny Farm he liked so much.

"With all that settled, they probably pinned a note on Stool saying that he was the murderer and then told him to go on up to the station and Kip's stooge, Ollie Taylor, would give him a cell and a confession to sign. Rupe Hobson would then be up to defend him and see that the confession stuck."

It made sense. "But where were you all this time?" I said.

"At the hospital with Weenie," Delbert said. "Sam called me and said that he and Phil had lied about Kip threatening Rita— they had just been sore at him. The real murderer, he said, was Stool Williams. He had just staggered into the police station and confessed everything to Officer Ollie Taylor.

"Well, when he said that, I rushed down to throw Stool out of jail and Ollie in it but as soon as I went in the station there was Kip and Mr. Phelps. Kip must have figured on having trouble with us and, not knowing the hold you got over Mr. Phelps, he had brought him along to help out.

"He told him that we were trying to frame him for the murder with some lies we had heard and that was the reason that I didn't want to take Stool's confession. Well, Mr. Phelps slipped me a wink to let me know that he was still on our side and then he said that he thought Stool was guilty too but, as mayor, he hated to see such dissension in one of his departments so he would like to take the matter up with us this morning. And that's the way things stand right now and that meeting is where we're heading!"

And with that he started the car up but I stopped him again because I had the feeling he hadn't told me everything. And he hadn't. I asked him if he and Weenie had found anything else to connect Kip with the cab ride and he got this nasty, smug smile on his face like he was going to teach me a lesson for going off and leaving him.

"Yeah," he said real casually, "we found a little something to link him up with it."

I had to warn him again that I wasn't in the mood for jokes. "Now what is it?"

"Kip Belton's money clip!" he said. "We found it under the back seat of the cab and we know it's his because it's got his

initials on it and everybody in town has seen the show-off bastard flashing them hundred-dollar bills in it."

I tried acting casual too. "Where is it?"

"Hid in the lockbox in your desk. Along with an affidavit
from Weenie telling about his ride Saturday night and telling
about finding the clip under the seat when we were looking for
clues. He also says that it was the first time Kip Belton ever put
his fat butt in his cab. When I put a noose around a bastard's
neck, it fits him like a goiter. He ain't slipping out of it."

"But he don't know about it?"

"He don't know nothing. We gonna wait until he gets to
shooting off his big mouth about this confession and then we're
gonna take that clip and close that big mouth."

"You ain't told anybody?"

"I hinted about it to Dr. Winston. I did some more checking
on him and his alibi. When he left the hospital where that woman
was having the baby, he didn't just ride around like he said. He
went down to Sim's and had a sandwich and *then* he went riding
around. *He* could've heard Sam and Phil in that toilet talking
about Kip and Rita too and then rode out to Rita's himself. I told
him all that but I also told him that Weenie might be able to clear
him so he sure'n hell better not let him die. That's the reason he
ain't left Weenie's bedside since he was hit. He's hovering over
him like a bull angel."

As homely as Delbert was I almost wanted to kiss him.
Everything was turning out just like I hoped it would. All we
had to do was confront Kip with that clip and Weenie's affidavit
and he'd know there wouldn't be any use bringing Lacey into the
case. Mama and them were safe at last.

"Let's go!" I said.

He cut loose with the siren and we headed up Dock Street
at sixty miles an hour. It was one of the wildest rides I ever took
and it had the usual affect on Delbert. With everybody duck-
ing into alleys and running up on sidewalks getting out of his

way, it made him power mad. When we pulled up in front of the City Hall and all the members of the Sitting and Spitting Society rushed out to see what was happening, he laid into 'em.

"Back, you damn vultures!" he bellowed. "Back!"

I apologized to everybody for his conduct and then we went inside and went back to the Council room where he said Mr. Phelps and Kip and Rupe were waiting for us. I started to knock on the door but he kicked it open and Mr. Phelps and them, who were sitting around this big table, nearly fell out of their chairs.

"Damnit, Delbert," Kip roared, "you come in here right. This ain't any whore house you're raiding."

"It ain't?" Delbert sneered. "From the jazzing you're trying to give me and Buck, I thought it was, you murdering bastard."

Kip nearly came across the table at him. "By God, Sam Bates *told* you that he was lying about me threatening that slut. I was in bed with my wife at midnight and she'll tell you I was. Now you apologize for that!"

I knew right then that he had got the call from Lacey saying she would back him up. Delbert sat down and gave a nasty laugh and then made an even nastier remark about what Kip could do with an apology. Mr. Phelps started pounding on the table and pleading for quiet. He said that we were all his boys and it just broke his heart to see such dissension.

"Now, Brother Peters," he sighed at me, "will you lead us in a few words of prayer, asking God's guidance on these proceedings?"

That was another thing that annoyed me about him. In private he was always calling me a conniving sonofabitch, but in public he was always asking me to pray for him. He knew how I hated being sacrilegious and that's what it was. But I prayed.

"Amen!" he said, as though he hadn't been studying Kip's face and chuckling to himself the whole time I was praying.

"Now, Chief Peters, I suppose Officer Tate here has filled you in on the details surrounding Mr. Stool Williams's confession?"

I said he had. "And you agree with him?" he said. "You think that Stool just imagines he's the murderer?"

"Well, in something this serious," I said, "I think we ought to be dead sure he *ain't* just imagining it."

"Exactly why we're here!" he said.

Then he got real civic again. He said that he knew that, as mayor, he didn't have any business interfering with the due processes of the law but that the police department was part of his administration and he would sure appreciate it if we would agree to let him arbitrate the case. After all, he was a lot older and more experienced than we were and he had always tried being a second father to us and it would sure warm his heart if we would let him act in that capacity for us at this time.

Well, that was pretty nauseating but I agreed to abide by his decision and so did Rupe, and Kip smiled real big and said that he would too, that he had always regarded Mr. Phelps as the Grand Old Man of Greenhill and he hadn't ever seen him make a mistake yet.

What he meant was that Mr. Phelps must know that he and Sam and Phil had made a deal with Stool and being as how they were big shots in town he wouldn't make the mistake of messing them up because he would want their continued support on civic matters. What he didn't know was that Mr. Phelps had been laying for 'em and was going to get *all* their heads in a single noose and be *guaranteed* their continued support.

He acted like he was real touched by Kip's tribute though, and then he got down to business.

"Now, the way I understand it," he said. "Stool Williams staggered into the station here yesterday afternoon and confessed to Officer Oliver Taylor that, because of some past grievance, he had emptied a gun into Rita Singleton's bedroom early Sunday morning and murdered her. He was jailed, his confession drawn up and out of that came this difference of opinion. Am I correct?"

"You are, sir!" Rupe said.

"Well, Mr. Hobson," Mr. Phelps said real quick and loud to drown out more of Delbert's obscene mutterings, "suppose we hear your side of the case first."

Rupe cleared his throat and got to his feet. He was a big, bald-headed, pouchy fellow about seventy. He had big pouches under his eyes and big pouches at the bottom of his cheeks, and under his chin he had such a pouch he could've been carrying his young in his mouth. He did all Kip's legal work which meant that he had to do all Kip's illegal work too. He was a great actor though. He looked so sad and solemn you would have thought he was defending himself.

"Mr. Mayor, Commissioner Belton, Chief Peters... I am here today to defend Stool Williams. As you all know Stool Williams is a thief, an alcoholic, a peeping-tom and a sex maniac."

"Now, by God," Delbert blurted out, "that's what I call a bang-up job of defending."

Rupe sighed and ignored him and kept on going. He said that Stool had been in the asylum three times and that there was no crime that his diseased brain wasn't capable of concocting. Therefore he wasn't going to try and delude any jury into thinking that Stool wasn't a murderer. All he was going to do was plead insanity for him and try and get him shipped off for treatment.

"So, I respectfully request, Mr. Mayor, that you require your officers to accept this confession, cease their efforts to lay the blame elsewhere, put this poor devil away and spare him any more of the torture that he must be suffering at this moment. Thank you for your attention, gentlemen."

With that he sat down. Kip gave him an approving look and Mr. Phelps beamed like he thought he had done a good job too. What he was beaming about, though, was the thought of having Rupe's head in the noose with the rest of 'em.

"Well, Chief Peters," he drawled, "Mr. Hobson's request seems reasonable enough. You got anything to say."

I got to my feet and said that I would like to ask Stool a question, if nobody minded. Kip minded right off. He said there wasn't any use asking him any damn questions, that everything was in the confession.

I had figured on that. They hadn't planned on him talking to anybody until the trial. Then Bo McWhorter, the County Prosecutor, who had two brothers and a cousin working in Kip's plant, would ask Stool if he was guilty and Stool would say sure, and a jury of twelve husbands who had been running after Rita, would retire for thirty seconds of deliberating, and the case would be closed.

"But, Kip," I said, "all I want is for Stool, himself, to tell me that he did it. That's the only question I'll ask him about the confession."

He looked real suspicious and so did Rupe but Mr. Phelps gave them a big comforting smile like I couldn't do any harm with just that one question. "Well, I don't think anybody can object to that. I certainly don't want people saying I didn't hear both sides of the case."

Kip nodded like he appreciated Mr. Phelps making everything look so legal and Delbert went out and got Stool out of his cell and brought him in and sat him down at the end of the table.

I felt real sorry for him. Mama had told me how he had been born out of wedlock and his mother, before she died, had farmed him out from one place to the other when he was a little boy. He'd been about three-quarter-witied then, but with everybody making fun of him he just got worse. Then he found out about whisky and the kind he drank just about finished off his brain.

Now he was about fifty but looked about seventy because most of his teeth were gone and his face was all white and pasty and what with being so thin and bony he looked like a dressed chicken. He was just pitiful. But he was grinning at me with them five bad teeth he had in front, and that was what counted.

"Stool," I said, real friendly, "you know who I am?"

Before he could answer, Rupe boiled to his feet. "I object! I won't have a client of mine brain-washed this way."

"But, Rupe," Mr. Phelps sighed, "he just asked him if he ..."

"He was going to ask him just *one* question! He's trying to confuse him. My client is a murderer and he's not going to be talked out of it."

Kip told him to please sit down. He had got a signal from Mr. Phelps that Rupe was going to mess everything up if he kept on. Rupe sighed and gave Kip a "don't-blame-me-then" look and sat down. I asked Stool again if he knew who I was.

"Sure, Buck," he said, "I know you."

"You know this fellow?" I said, pointing to Delbert.

His grin got even wider and wetter then. "Sure, Buck, that's old Delbert."

"Well, Stool," I said, "I'm sure glad you remember us because I was kind of getting the impression you had forgot us."

He looked sort of embarrassed at that, like I was teasing him. "Aw, Buck, I wouldn't never forget you and old Delbert, you know that?"

"Why not?"

"Because you're my friends, Buck. You and old Delbert, the best friends I got."

That brought Rupe to his feet again. "By God, Phelps, I just won't have a client of mine tortured this way!"

Kip didn't seem to care for the turn things were taking either but Mr. Phelps gave him that comforting look again and he frowned for Rupe to stop interrupting me and I started in again.

"Now, Stool," I said, "you say that old Delbert and I are the best friends you've got. What makes you say that? I can't think of anything we ever did for you."

That got him embarrassed again. "Aw, Buck, you're always helping me. You even saved my life, you and old Delbert!"

"You mean that night down in Mill Town?" I said.

He acted just the way I hoped he would. He licked his lips and nodded and hunched forward in his chair like he wanted to be closer to me.

"Now, Stool," I said, "that was the night you went down in Mill Town and got caught peeping in Thelma Taylor's bedroom window, wasn't it?"

He nodded.

"And when Delbert and I got down there," I said, "about half the folks in Mill Town had you out in the street arguing over what to do with you. Bailey Thomas..." I stopped and asked him if he remembered Bailey. He mumbled that he did and the sweat started popping out on his forehead. Bailey weighed about two-fifty and he had had Stool by the neck.

"And, Stool," I said, "Bailey wanted to throw you off the rail-road trestle into the river but Stoney Dykes wanted to strip you naked and beat you through the streets. Thelma, though, wanted to hang you on the spot. Then what happened?"

The tears started welling up in his eyes. "You saved my life," he sniffed. "You hit Bailey and Stoney and Delbert hit Thelma."

"Well," I said, "when you were clinging to my legs and trying to kiss my hands, didn't you say all sorts of things about how you were going to pay me and old Delbert back?"

Rupe sighed and Kip cut his eyes at Mr. Phelps. Mr. Phelps cut his eyes back at him like he wasn't sure he had ever seen him before and then he concentrated on Stool. Stool sniffed and said that he had meant every word he'd said about paying me and old Delbert back for helping him out. There wasn't anything in the world he wouldn't do for us. I eased around the table and put my arm around him.

"Well, then tell me something," I said. *"Did you kill Rita Singleton?"*

The change of pace was too much for his poor mind. One second he was in Mill Town, the next second he was at Rita Singleton's and he couldn't make the switch that fast. Kip and Rupe weren't positive of it though, so they didn't scream, they just sat there staring at him like a couple of cobras hypnotized by a scrawny old bird. Stool blinked a couple of times like there was something he ought to remember about Rita but then he gave it up.

"Kill Rita Singleton?" he said, grinning real foolish. "Why would I want to kill Rita, Buck? She was my friend. She used to wink at me. I wouldn't kill her."

For a second there wasn't a sound, then Rupe acted like he was shocked beyond words. "I'll be damned!" he gasped. "The idiot did just imagine all that."

"Get the smelly bastard out of here!" Kip snarled.

I knew what they were up to. Blame the whole thing on Stool's imagination and get him out of the way before he got them messed up in it. Delbert and Mr. Phelps knew that's what they were trying to do and they were loving it but not as much as I was. All I had to do was finish clearing Stool, get them implicated, and then, when Kip started bellowing, pull Weenie's affidavit and the money clip on him.

"Well, Stool," I drawled, "just what did you do Saturday night?"

I wanted to get that on record first, in case he tried changing his story, then I would work into Sunday afternoon and Kip and them and their confession. Stool's face lit up and then it fell.

"You won't get mad at me, Buck? I remember what I done Saturday night but one thing wasn't so good!"

Now for a second that gave me a start but then I figured out what he must be talking about.

"Stool," I said, "haven't I told you that if you come and tell me everything bad you do, it might not be as hard on you and I'd try to help you?"

That was the arrangement we had. One of those man-to-man things. Nobody else knew anything about it. I could almost feel the vibrations from Kip's cringing. He sure hadn't known anything about it. Stool started grinning.

"That's right! If I steal anything from a store, you take it back for me, don't you?"

"That's right!" I said. "Now what did you do Saturday night?"

"Well," he said, "the bad thing I did was peep in a window at Mr. Kip's house!"

Well, I felt like a beagle that had been trailing a rabbit and all of a sudden had come across a wildcat. The wildcat was Kip Belton's house on Saturday night. I didn't know what Stool was going to say about it but I just preferred not to have it in the conversation at all.

"Well, maybe Mr. Kipp will excuse you!" I said, real fast, not even stopping to see how the others would take it. "Now what else were you doing?"

He started to answer but good old Delbert and his big mouth drowned him out. "Now just a second here!" he said. "What about you peeping in the Beltons' window?" He seemed to have caught the scent of a wildcat or something too.

"Delbert," I snapped, "we ain't here to discuss the invasion of people's privacy. All we're trying to do right now is clear Stool of this murder!"

"Well, it ain't all I'm trying to do," he said, "and don't you go getting godly on me. Stool, what time did you peep in that window?"

"Delbert, how would he know?" I said. "And what difference does it make? You sound like a dirty little boy trying to find out what goes on in the little girls' toilet!"

"Deacon, will you shut up," he said. "All I asked him was what time he peeped in the window. Now what time was it, Stool?"

"Lemme think!" Stool said. "I know but I got to think."

I cut my eyes at Kip. He was about to go crazy. He was trying to figure out about three things at the same time. Had Mr. Phelps double-crossed him, what was Delbert up to, and what time had Stool peeked in his windows? He was trying to cover all that confusion up by grinning like he thought it was a good joke, Stool peeking in his windows. He just looked nauseated though.

"Well," Stool said, "it was after the western let out at the picture show."

I groaned inside but Delbert brightened considerably. "Well, the picture show lets out at eleven-thirty on Saturday nights so…"

Stool brightened too. "It was after midnight I did it," he said, "because I walked out Main Street and just as I was turning down River Road I heard the town clock strike twelve and I know it was twelve because I always count it clean around."

"I see!" Delbert said. "So it was after midnight. Now what window did you peep in?"

"Delbert," I said, "are you just trying to embarrass Stool?" I turned to Stool. "Stool, don't you realize that's Mr. Kip sitting there and you ought not to be talking this way."

"I know it's Mr. Kip, Buck!" he whined. "I want him to know I didn't mean to peep in his window but I couldn't help it. I saw this light in this bedroom window and I got to thinking about how pretty Miss Lacey was and I just couldn't…"

I beat on the table. "By George!" I shouted. "I just won't have it. I won't have a fine girl brought into…"

"Damn it, will you stop acting like a deacon," Delbert roared, "and start acting like a chief of police? Now what did you see, Stool? Did you see Miss Lacey?"

I rolled my eyes at Kip and wanted to kill him. He was too scared to say anything. Not Stool, though. Not even with all my hollering. It was like Delbert had him hypnotized.

"Yeah," he said. "I saw Miss Lacey! But she wasn't naked, Mr. Kip."

That didn't seem to cheer up Kip any more than it did me.

"You mean she had all her clothes on?" Delbert said real insinuatingly.

"Naw," Stool said, "she had on these little short white pants and a shirt and ..."

"Pajamas, you mean?" Delbert said.

"I guess so," Stool said. "And she sat down in front of this mirror and was singing something and dabbing something behind her ears and ..."

I started screaming about the indecency of it all but Stool said he hadn't seen anything bad and then Delbert busted in again.

"Hell, Stool, you don't have to tell Mr. Kip you didn't see anything bad. Wasn't he in bed watching her?"

"Naw," Stool grinned. "There wasn't nobody in the bedroom but her. The bed wasn't even messed up."

Kip started coming to life then, but just barely. I heard him gasp to Mr. Phelps that Stool was crazy. Delbert heard him too but he didn't holler at him. A dog don't bay when he's right on top of what he's chasing. He just turned to Kip and said all right, maybe Stool was crazy but please let him finish. That trapped Kip for good. He *thought* he knew what everybody was thinking but nobody had accused him of anything so all he could do was just sit there trying to think of what to say when they *did* accuse him of something.

"Now, Stool," Delbert said, "you're positive there wasn't anybody in the bed? What about in the room?"

"There wasn't anybody in the room. She went out back."

I gave up and Delbert didn't seem too happy either. He seemed to think that Stool really had started imagining things.

"It was after midnight," he said, "and she went out back? In her pajamas?"

"She sure did!" Stool said. "She left the room and I waited for her to come back but then I heard a door slammed and I sneaked around back and I could see her skipping down the back lawn into the garden. She was so pretty I sneaked down through the shrubbery to watch her some more but then I got scared and went home to bed."

"You got scared?" Delbert wheezed, as though he was wondering just what he had come up with. "Why?"

"Because," Stool said, "there was a man in the garden with Miss Lacey!"

CHAPTER NINE

WELL, when Stool topped off his recital by saying that Lacey was in the garden with a man, Kip jumped even higher than I did and started across the table at Delbert. He screeched that Delbert had put Stool up to it.

"He's a liar and you know it!"

Rupe and Mr. Phelps grabbed him and while he was trying to bull his way loose I wrestled Delbert over into a corner and told him to forget Stool, that a halfwit's testimony wouldn't stand up in court, especially if he was trying to tell people that Lacey Belton was running around in her pajamas at midnight with another man.

"Won't anybody believe that," I whispered, "and you know they won't!"

"By God, I believe it," he said, "and I'm gonna find out who the sneaky sonofabitch was and then we won't have to count on drunks and half-wits to prove that she wasn't in bed with this fat bastard. We find him and this case is busted wide open!" He started trying to get loose again and yelled over at Kip, "Belton, I want to talk to that wife of yours."

"You white-trash sonofabitch," Kip yelled back, "I better not ever catch you near my wife!"

"Well, somebody's been near her. What were they doing, Stool?"

I slapped one hand over Stool's mouth and told him we'd had enough of his irresponsible talk and with my other hand I gave Delbert a shake. I told him that he was a fine police officer but he just couldn't go insinuating such things about a fine, innocent girl like Lacey Belton.

"There must be some explanation for this so we'll just go up there and talk to her."

It was the only thing I could think of. Lacey was still at the lodge and, if I took them to the Belton house instead, it would give me time to think.

"All right," Delbert said, "we'll go but *I'll* do the talking!" He said that finding out what a man and a woman were doing in a garden at midnight wasn't any job for a deacon. "She could tell you they were out there potting petunias and you'd believe her."

"But she wasn't in any garden!" Kip screeched.

"But, Mr. Kip, she was!" Stool whined. "The man was about the size of..."

I slapped my hand over his mouth again and Mr. Phelps got back into things. He put his arm around Kip's shoulder and drooled, "Son, why don't *I* talk to her?"

Kip slapped at the arm like it was a snake. "Because you're a mealy-mouth old pig. I'm gonna let this lint-head sonofabitch here talk to her and, by God, he's gonna believe her."

Delbert and Mr. Phelps both started talking at once. Delbert said he sure was gonna believe her because he knew how to get the truth out of women and Mr. Phelps said that if he had been accused of murder he'd think twice before he called anybody a mealy-mouth old pig and that's when I broke it up. I told Mr. Phelps to go into Stool's confession a little deeper with him and Rupe, and then I told Delbert and Kip to go outside and wait for me, that I wanted to call Mama to let her know I was all right.

They went on out and I went in my office and closed the door and got down on one knee and prayed. I told the Lord that it wasn't for myself that I was beseeching his aid, it was for Mama and them, and if He was counting on my taking over the county and bringing liberty, justice and Jesus to all, He had better help His humble servant and help him fast.

It was like a miracle. No sooner did I say amen and get up off my knee than this great light seemed to dawn on me and this voice inside me seemed to say, "Call the Beltons'. Talk to Pert." And that's what I did. I called the Beltons' number and Pert answered and I didn't give her a chance to say a thing. I told her that Delbert and I were coming up to question Lacey about Kip not being in bed at midnight and her being out in the garden with a man.

"And I don't want any distractions from you," I said, "and I mean it."

She tried to say something but I slammed down the phone and went outside and joined Kip and Delbert. Kip headed for his own car and Delbert tried to stop him, but I told him it would be all right just so long as Kip followed us. That made him mad but it made Delbert even madder. We got in the squad car and he started raving that I never was gonna make a chief of police, I was just too nice to people.

"That's the reason *I'm* gonna handle Lacey!" he said. It was gonna break my heart, he said, finding out that my old girl was out tomcatting with somebody but I was gonna be a better policeman for it. "You just watch the way I handle women!"

He kept on raving about how the main thing was not to let women distract you with their looks and the airs they put on. By the time he had finished his lecture we had lost Kip at a stop light. About five minutes later we turned up the Belton driveway, wound up through the pines and parked around behind the house. We got out and Delbert tried acting like he wasn't impressed with the place and then he hitched up his pistol belt like he was going to take it over.

"You wait for that bastard," he said, meaning Kip. "I'll go in and get her."

He swaggered off toward the house but he never reached it. Halfway across the patio he stopped, gaped at something, and then started quivering like a bird dog on a point. The shrubbery kept me from seeing what he was gaping at so I started walking toward him. He still didn't move, he just kept standing there vibrating. Then I was clear of the shrubbery and could see what had set up all his vibrations and in that second I knew that the Lord had heard my prayers.

It was Pert. She was stretched out on a lawn chair like a siren on a rock and didn't have a thing on but a little white sun suit that fit her like a skin graft. Delbert thought she was asleep but he ought've known every thing was arranged too tidy and tormenting.

One leg was out flat but the other one was cocked up so as to show off about a yard of white meat. And the sun suit was the kind held up by a string around the neck but she didn't have it held up. It was at half mast and Delbert looked like he thought her breasts were gonna jump out at him.

And in addition to all that, she had on some perfumed sort of oil that put a golden sheen to her skin and what with her silky, black hair glistening in the sun and her breasts rising and falling I could understand how a boy with a mind like Delbert's might be impressed.

But I walked up to him like I didn't even see Pert "What's the matter with you?" I said.

"Buck," he whimpered, "you hold her for me and I'll hold her for you. So help me God, I'll…"

This real loud, nasty voice behind us drowned him out. "Pert, for God's sake, go put some clothes on!"

It was Kip. He had parked up behind us and for some reason neither one of us had heard him. Pert gave a jump like he had woke her up and then she snatched the top of her sun suit up and laughed and said, "Well, what's *this* all about?"

She directed the question at me like she would teach me to give her orders over the phone but I ignored it and so did Kip. He elbowed me and Delbert aside and told Pert to go in the house and put some clothes on and tell Lacey to come out.

Pert just grinned and tied the string of the sun suit around her neck but made sure that she didn't tie it tight. She said that Lacey wasn't home. "And I'm not telling you where she is until you tell me what this is all about!"

"Is she still at that damn lodge?" Kip said.

Pert ignored him and got to her feet like a cobra coming out of a basket and came toward Delbert like she was stalking him. Kip started to bellow for her to go on in the house but then he saw the look on Delbert's face. Pert planted herself right in front of him, clasped her hands behind her back, stuck her breasts out and smiled up at him, "You'll tell me, won't you, Delbert?"

Delbert tried to get his mind back on his duties and demonstrate his woman-handling technique, but Pert didn't have a thing under that sun suit but her.

"Aw, it ain't anything much," he wheezed. "That fool, Stool Williams, just told us some wild story about how he peeped in a window up here Saturday night and says he didn't see Kip in bed with Lacey, he saw her out in the garden with a man."

That's when Pert made me and Kip break out in a cold sweat too. She laughed and said that Stool was right, he *hadn't* seen Kip in bed—at least not in the bedroom he had peeped in—and he *had* seen Lacey in the garden with a man, but it wasn't what we thought.

"Everybody sit down," she grinned, "and I'll tell you all about it." She prissed back to the lawn chair and sat down, and then reached up and pulled Delbert down with her. "You sit here with me and tell me all about it."

She was leaning toward him and with that sun suit hanging loose he could see just about all of her breasts. He looked like a man with lockjaw staring in a bakery window.

"Hunh?" he said. I didn't think that was too brilliant a question for a man who could handle women but I didn't say anything.

"I said, 'tell me what Stool said.' " Pert smiled.

"Who?" Delbert said.

"Stool!" I said, real patiently. "Stool Williams. Pert wants you to tell her just what Stool said he saw!"

"Oh, *him!*" he said. "Well, old Stool said that…" He gave a big sigh and wiped the sweat from his face with his arm and wheezed, "Maybe you'd better tell her, Buck!"

Well, that salted him away and Pert turned on me. When she had been looking at Delbert her eyes had a twinkle in 'em but now they had that same strange gleam they'd had the day before when she'd told me to stop acting like a deacon. I started in telling her what Stool had said. She looked real amused about Kip not being in bed and when I came to the part about Lacey being in the garden with a man she started laughing.

"The Iron Maiden with a lover! That's the funniest thing I ever heard!" Then she finally stopped torturing us. "That wasn't a man, that was *me!*"

I gave almost as big a sigh as Kip did and it even brought Delbert back with us for a second.

"You?" he gasped. "He mistook *you* for a man?"

Pert laughed some more and pinched his cheek and sent him back into his trance and then said sure, it was her. It seemed that Lacey hadn't been able to get to sleep Saturday night so she had asked her, Pert, to go out in the garden and have a cigarette. She had said all right, but before she went she had put on some slacks and a golf jacket, in case there were any mosquitoes.

Then when they got in the garden they'd discovered that neither of 'em had a match so Lacey had come back to the house.

"And you know how silly she can be sometimes," Pert said. "She's got this perfume that she thinks keeps mosquitoes away so she put some of it on before she came back to the garden. Stool followed her, I suppose, saw my slacks and golf jacket and thought I was a man. Isn't that priceless?"

Well, for a lie that she hadn't had more than ten minutes to cook up, it wasn't too bad. Of course a policeman with Delbert's knack for handling women could have picked it to pieces, but he was too busy staring down into the sun suit.

So I cut my eyes at Kip to see how he was taking it. As near as I could tell, his ego had him running true to form. The man in the garden really was Pert, he thought, and she was lying about him being at home because he was her brother and such a swell fellow. I changed the subject slightly.

"Well, Pert," I drawled, "I figured it was something like that or else Stool was just having one of his spells, but what about him saying that Kip wasn't in the bedroom?"

"He wasn't!" she laughed. "Stool was peeping in a *guest room* window. Lacey just stopped by there to put on the perfume. She didn't want to disturb Kip. He was asleep in their bedroom across the hall and didn't even know Lacey was up."

"Well, that takes care of that," I said, and gave Delbert a punch. "You got any more questions?"

He came out of his coma with a jump and then real brightly said no, he didn't have anything else to say except that he wanted to apologize to Kip for all his accusations. Then he gave Pert a real sickening smile and told her she didn't have a thing to worry about. "Old Delbert's gonna take care of everything, honey, including you!"

He made it sound like Pert just couldn't wait to get him in a motel. Kip wanted to kill him but instead he patted him on the back and helped him to his feet and said there weren't any hard feelings, that he knew he had just been doing his duty and it was a pleasure to watch such a fine, wide-awake policeman at work.

With that Pert got up, all smiles, and took Delbert by the hand and led him off toward the car, telling him how cute he always looked in his uniform and why didn't he call her some time. Kip looked like he was going after Delbert but just then Ormond, the butler, came out and said that he was wanted on the phone. He gave me one last glare and started in the house. I watched him and got to wondering what he was really thinking and then, out of the corner of my eye, I saw Pert coming toward me and I got to wondering what *she* was really thinking.

If she didn't really know what had happened in the garden and had just been covering up for Kip then why did she have that gleam in her eye and why was she coming at me the same way she had come at Delbert? I figured it was just my conscience.

"Don't go flaunting your charms at me," I said, trying to get past her. "You ought to be ashamed of yourself treating that boy the way you did."

She grinned and planted herself right in my path. "It won't work, Deacon," she said. "It's your time to flaunt your charms. *Just like you did with Lacey in the garden Saturday night.*"

There wasn't a thing to do but try and bluff her. I got real aghast. *"What* are you talking about?" I said.

"I'll give you a sample," she said and with that she sort of tilted her head back and got a real passionate look on her face and whimpered, "Don't stop, Buck. Don't stop." I knew right then she wasn't just guessing. She had been in the garden and she had been close enough to hear Lacey. I kept trying to bluff her though.

"You're crazy!" I said. "You just said that *you* were in the garden with …"

I was drowned out by Delbert blowing the horn. Pert's grin disappeared and she looked down at her watch and got real grim and businesslike. She told me that at one o'clock she was going to start out on a little walk down to the river. I was going to pick her up along River Road.

"We're going out to the lodge to see Lacey!" she said.

I gave up. "But what about?" I whimpered.

"About my price for keeping quiet!"

CHAPTER TEN

WELL, at 12:30 I was in my office talking to Mama on the phone and it was like talking to a duck because she was full of gossip about the case and was just quacking away. She said that she had heard that we were about to arrest Elmer Bell because Weenie had seen him coming out of Rita's side road around three o'clock Sunday morning and that was the reason Elmer had run over Weenie with his lumber truck.

"And that's the reason you've got Dr. Winston nursing Weenie so!" she said. "He's your chief witness."

I straightened that out for her. I told her that Elmer had been down in Louisiana Sunday morning and besides that he hadn't run into Weenie, Weenie had run into him.

"As for Dr. Winston," I said, "he is looking after Weenie because he might die. I talked to him not twenty minutes ago and he still don't know whether Weenie is going to make it or not. He's still unconscious."

Which was the truth and Dr. Winston was all scared because Delbert had told him that he looked like he was our chief suspect again, what with Pert having given Kip an alibi.

"Well, I know one thing for certain," Mama said. "A certain group of prominent citizens got up a hundred thousand dollars and gave it to Stool Williams to sign that confession. I understand that the Chamber of Commerce put up five thousand of it to save the town's name."

"They didn't do any such thing," I said. "Stool told Mr. Phelps this morning that Sam Bates and Phil Gaunt and Kip Belton paid him twenty dollars and two bottles of wine to sign that confession but they say that he's crazy and that if he didn't like the asylum so much they would have him put away."

"Maybe I've got it mixed up," she said. "Maybe the hundred thousand was what a group got up to buy Rita's diary back. I understand that's what she got murdered for, wasn't it?"

"Mama, I got to go!" I said.

"Kip Belton did it, didn't he?" she said. "I hear that Rita had already blackmailed him for a half million dollars."

"Mama," I said, "Lacey says Kip was in bed with her at the time of the murder. Pert backs her up and Delbert backs Pert up."

"What's wrong with Delbert?"

"Nothing more than usual," I said. "He's sitting right here. He had a little talk with Pert about Kip, that's all. Now I got to go!"

She sighed and said all right, but to be sure and call Reverend Samuels, that he wanted me to make a talk before the Young People's Christian Union about the case. He thought it would be a good lesson for 'em. I told her I'd be sure and call him and then I told her good-by and hung up. Delbert looked over at me and shook his head.

"I sure wish they'd quit picking on that poor boy!" he said. "He's as innocent as you are!"

He meant Kip and I wanted to hit him right in the mouth. He was still in that sexual trance that Pert had put him in and he was still convinced that she just couldn't wait to deprive him of his virtue and the only thing that could keep it from coming to pass was me pinning the murder on Kip. It just made me sick, a murderer being defended by a whole police department because the Chief was having relations with his wife and the Assistant Chief was wanting to have relations with his sister and the rest of the department was wanting to have relations with his money.

"Delbert," I sighed, "I'm gonna ride over to the hospital and check on Weenie again."

"All right," he said, "but if he's conscious tell him I think he's out of his mind about that money clip we found in his back seat. Somebody could've rolled Kip, got the money clip and then lost it in his cab."

Well, I didn't go to the hospital. I rode past it real slow and then I rode out Main Street real slow and, just as the town clock struck one, I turned on to River Road. Then just before I reached the Beltons', I saw Pert coming down the driveway.

She had her hair in a pony-tail and had on a tight white blouse and a swirly pink skirt and a near-sighted stranger might have thought she was little Bo-Peep, she looked so sweet and girlish. She swished on down the driveway, looked in the mail box and, as she did, I pulled up behind her.

"Before you get in here," I said, "where's Kip?"

She laughed and got in anyway. "He's gone to Memphis. He says it's on business but I'll bet he's after a lawyer."

"How you know he hasn't gone to the lodge instead?"

"What if he has?" she said. "We'll tell him that you've just brought me out to check my story with Lacey. We won't tell him what we've *really* come out for!"

I sighed and started up the car and headed out the road. My last hope had been scaring her away from the lodge. She grinned and scooted over close to me and put her hand on my knee. It felt like a branding iron. "Now tell me all about it, Buck!" she said.

I wasn't going to tell her a thing but I didn't see any sense getting her riled up so I just took her hand off my knee and told her that she would have to tell me how she had caught us first. She laughed and said that it had been real simple and, if I hadn't been a deacon and Lacey a Sunday School teacher and we hadn't been so godly acting, she would have caught us before.

She said that she had come in from her date Saturday night and hadn't been able to sleep so she had started reading. Around one o'clock she had run out of cigarettes and started downstairs to get some more. Halfway down the stairs she had heard Lacey come in the back way. She was humming and seemed so happy about something that she, Pert, had got suspicious. She never had been able to understand what pleasure she could get out of sitting in that garden at night by herself.

So she, Pert, had kept real quiet and when she heard Lacey go back out she had watched her from an upstairs window. When she saw her practically dancing out into the garden she had got more suspicious and sneaked out into the garden herself.

"I had to be real quiet at first, Buck," she smirked, "but when you started making love to Lacey I didn't have to be quiet at all. I walked up within nearly ten feet of you and stood behind that big boxwood and watched you the whole time. I nearly went crazy. Especially when ..."

"Never mind!" I snapped and started going faster. She just grinned some more and said that it was my turn to tell her things. I told her that I wasn't going to tell her a thing, that I just couldn't understand how she could act the way she was, knowing that her brother was a murderer.

She just pooh-poohed that. She said that he hadn't killed Rita, that he'd never done anything in his life without somebody to help him and Saturday night he had been too drunk to kill anybody and that was *one* of the reasons she had lied for him.

"If I thought he really murdered her," she said, "you could have him, but I think it's funny. He probably thinks you've got him trapped or will have and you think he's got you trapped and you're both wrong. I'll bet on it."

Well, I could have told her about Kip practically admitting his guilt by trying to bribe Lacey with the million dollars and the divorce but, first, I wanted to see what else she might come up with. She wasn't long coming.

"Now," she said, "when was the first time you ever made love to Lacey?"

I just ignored her and started driving faster.

"Well, what's the *most* you've ever made love to her in one night? I know you made love to her three times Saturday night and I didn't get there until one o'clock! You were just fabulous. Honestly!"

It made me want to climb under the hood but I still didn't say anything, and she started laughing and put her head on my shoulder and said how cute I looked when I blushed, and how she wished Reverend Samuels and the ladies' choir could have been in the garden and seen their pet deacon in action. Then she reached up and bit me on the ear. Not hard. Just enough for me to catch the silky sweetness of her hair and the hot softness of her lips. I nearly ran off the road.

"If you don't get off me," I said, "and if you don't stop talking that way, you're gonna *walk* to that lodge!"

She turned my ear loose and started pouting. "Well, if you don't stop being so pious," she said, "I'll bite it clean off. Now say what you're thinking."

"I just told you what I was thinking!" I said. "I think you ought to be ashamed of yourself!"

"That's not what you're thinking! You're thinking how nice it would be, if you weren't all involved with Lacey and with playing the deacon, and we could pull into that side road down there and take the seat out and ..."

I finished it for her. "And lay you across it and give you a spanking!" I snapped. "That's all you're old enough for!"

She started getting mad. "Hold up your right hand!" she said. "Hold it up and *swear* that you don't want to make love to me."

"I swear it!" I said.

"You're lying! Your eyes wouldn't light up the way they do when you look at me, if you weren't lying!"

"Pert," I said, trying to be fatherly, "you just don't know what a horrible thing adultery is!"

"Well, Saturday night you didn't sound like it was so horrible. You sounded like it was the grandest thing that ..."

"Pert, I'm sorry," I said, "but you don't arouse anything in me but pity!"

She glared at me and started flicking her nails like a cat sharpening its claws. "Just keep talking!" she said.

I did. I kept talking clean down to the farm gate that guarded the road to the lodge and then I talked to her all the way down to the lodge itself. I told her how spoiled she was and how conceited she was, thinking that just because she had a pretty car and pretty clothes and a right pretty little face and body that she could have anything she wanted and even make Christians forget their principles. By the time I pulled up alongside Lacey's convertible behind the lodge, I had her so mad that she wouldn't even talk about me in the garden any more.

"*Now,*" I said, opening the door for her to get out, "what's this price you're gonna charge Lacey and me for keeping quiet about us?"

She slammed the car door shut and swished up the back steps to the lodge, flung the door open and started hollering for Lacey. I followed her. Lacey didn't answer. We checked the bedrooms, then the big living room, and still she didn't answer. She was either out on the river or was taking a walk. I didn't like it because I had worked up such a head of steam preaching to Pert that I didn't care what happened and wanted to get it over with. I sat down on the big couch in front of the fireplace and glared at her.

"You haven't answered my question," I said. "What's your price for keeping quiet about us?"

All of a sudden she didn't seem mad any more. She folded her arms across her chest and smiled at me.

"*You!*" she said.

"Me?" I said.

She strolled over like she was Tarzan's mate and had just bagged a lion or something pretty special. Then she smiled some more and put her finger on the tip of my nose and pushed.

"*You* are my price for keeping quiet, Deacon. You and Lacey are through. You are not going to be her lover any more you're going to be *my* lover!"

Well, truthfully, I had had a sneaking suspicion that her price might call for that kind of coin so I was something of a disappointment to her. Instead of screaming rape, I just gave her a bitter little laugh and told her that I was sorry but if exposing me and Lacey was what she had in mind she would have to stand in line.

"Lacey is even crazier than you are!" I said. "She *wants* people to know about us. She is going to get up at the trial herself and tell everybody that she wasn't in bed with Kip and never has been and that while he was out with Rita she was out in the garden with me. She thinks by telling them that and busting Kip's alibi and sending him to the chair where he belongs, she will get her revenge on you Beltons. And by telling everybody that she has been a wife to him in name only, she thinks that will clear her of having married him in the first place. So, if you go around shooting off your mouth about me being her lover, you'll just be backing up her story and she will thank you kindly."

Now that stopped her cold and, while she stood there staring at me, I told her everything. I told her about Kip trying to bribe Lacey with the million dollars and the divorce, and about Weenie and the cab ride, and how Lacey would probably bad-mouth me into arresting Kip as soon as he got back from Memphis.

"All I've been doing," I said, "is stalling for time hoping that Weenie would regain consciousness and that Lacey would change her mind and let Weenie break his alibi instead of her. With the kind of price you're asking, though, she's just gonna laugh at both of us. Kip's going to the chair and I'm going to the Foreign Legion."

Now I thought the shock of knowing that her brother really was the murderer would bring her back to her senses and make her stop acting the way she was doing, but it didn't. She *still* didn't believe he was the murderer. She said he just didn't have the nerve to murder anybody because he would be too afraid of what would happen if he got caught.

"*But,*" she said, "if he could murder somebody, knowing that nothing would happen to him if he got caught, he'd do it in a second. And what would happen to him if he murdered you and Lacey? Nothing! What happened to Joe Shackleford?"

I could see what she was getting at. Joe Shackleford had caught Sweeny Johnson and his wife, Mrs. Shackleford, that is, in adultery, and had murdered them. The jury had been out just long enough for everybody to have a smoke and then had come back in and turned Joe loose and congratulated him.

"And," Pert said, "Sweeny at least had the decency to take Joe's wife to a motel. He didn't take her out in Joe's own back yard. *And,* if Kip kills you and Lacey, there won't be any chance of hanging Rita's murder on him—which he didn't do anyway—because you and Lacey are the only ones who can wreck his alibi. That lawyer he'll bring in from Memphis with him will make Weenie and Stool sound like idiots and all I've got to do is take a deep breath and wiggle at Delbert and he can't even talk."

"You're forgetting one thing!" I said. "Kip won't be murdering anybody because he'll be in jail."

"You hope he'll be in jail!" she said. "Maybe I'll see him first and tell him about you and Lacey or maybe his lawyer can get him *out* of jail!"

That was a point. If we couldn't book him on anything but suspicion of murder he *would* be able to get out on bail. I wasn't afraid for myself but I was for Lacey and if she moved in with me and my mother there really would be talk. In short, if there was some slip-up and he found out about us and got the chance to kill her, he wouldn't think twice about it.

"Pert," I said, "you're forgetting one other thing. You know good and well that you won't risk my life or Lacey's either one telling Kip about us. You're not that hard!"

For a second her eyes softened. She knew I had her. But then she realized that she had me too.

"Well, you aren't that hard either!" she snapped. "I'm prettier than Lacey, I've got a better figure and I'm cuter than she is and I've been throwing myself at you since I was ten years old and I don't care if you are a deacon and do love Lacey, you can be nice to me just once. You aren't that mean!"

"Pert," I said, "I don't want to be mean but …"

"Then don't be. Love me just one time like you loved Lacey and I'll never say another word. About anything. To Lacey or anybody. I promise."

Well, I couldn't think of myself, I had to think of Lacey. It could mean saving her life from that maniac. Besides, it wouldn't take long and it might not be what Pert expected and she might leave Lacey and me alone forever and maybe sex, too. And, if I didn't do it, she might not tell Kip but she'd be sure to tell Lacey what she had heard and seen in the garden and would rub it in so that Lacey would get so mad and be so intent on breaking the news first that she'd race into town and just start blabbing it to everybody.

So I didn't answer Pert right away. I went outside and looked all around and didn't see Lacey any place. Then I walked out to the steps leading down to the dock and didn't see her boat any place. It could have been in the boat-house but I figured that wasn't likely. She must be out on the river, which would give me enough time. I went back into the living room and glared at Pert.

"Just this one time?" I said.

She knew she had me then and she started acting like her old self again. "That's strictly up to you!" she smirked. The implication was that it was going to be habit forming.

"All right," I said, "but you're going to sign a paper saying that you forced me into this and that I'm doing it just to protect Lacey. She may walk in here and I ain't having you telling her some bragging lie about how this was all my idea."

She grinned at the thought of Lacey walking in and then she said that she would sign on one condition, that I wouldn't hold back or act like it was a duty dance. "You'll act like I'm Lacey!"

Well, that was pretty ridiculous but I told her all right and got out my pencil and pad and put it on my knee and started writing out my clearance paper. I started out: "I, Pert Belton, hereby swear that..." and that was about all I consciously remembered writing because Pert planted herself right in front of me and started doing a strip-tease.

First, she unbuttoned her blouse real slow and then slid it off her shoulders and let it fall. It hung on my knee for a second and I stopped writing and stared at it like it was a snake and then it dropped to the floor. I couldn't help looking up and, when I did, I couldn't help thinking about Delbert. It would have just drove him berserk. She had on a bra but it was one of those fancy, low-cut, streamlined kind and, instead of looking like it was restraining anything, it looked more like it was serving them up on a platter.

Well, I forced myself back to my writing but I couldn't tear one eye away from her hands. They fumbled with the zipper on her shorts and then there was a zip that made me feel like my throat getting cut and then she started peeling them down real slow. Then she stopped and said, real motherly like, "Buck, why don't you write on your little pad? You're writing all over your pants leg, honey!"

I was, too, but I ignored her and got back on the pad and she let her shorts fall. I quivered so that I broke my pencil point. She had on little, satiny, pink pants and you couldn't fault her any place. Her waist wasn't any bigger than a fruit jar and her hips and legs were... well, she stepped out of the shorts and it was like Venus stepping out of her oyster shell. I shoved the paper at her that I had finally finished writing out.

"Put your claw marks on that!" I said.

She laughed and took it and plopped down on the couch right beside me. I waited until she signed it and then I stuffed it in my pocket and jumped to my feet. Being on the same couch with her was like being on a launching pad.

"Which bedroom you want?" I said.

"I don't want any bedroom yet!" she pouted and with that she grabbed my hand and pulled me back down on the couch. I tried bouncing back up again but she had me off balance. The next thing I knew she had my head pinned against the back of the couch, kissing me.

Now I tried being just as cold and Spartan and loyal to Lacey as I could but Pert had lips like curling irons. Not that they weren't soft, they were like honey and velvet, but they heated up your head so that you could feel your hair beginning to get a set in it. And your ears too. The next thing I knew I was kissing her back and when that happened I figured the best thing I could do was try and get everything over with right there.

So I tried forcing her back on the couch but I couldn't do it because I was getting weaker by the second and she wasn't. All of my strength seemed to be flowing into her and, when the maneuvering was all over, she had me with my head resting on the arm of the couch and she was practically on top of me, still kissing me.

For a second I struggled but the next second I had my arms around her, kissing her back. Then it happened. I heard a sound. I thought at first it was just my ears popping. Then I heard it again. I opened one eye. For a second, I thought Pert had driven me out of my mind. The closet door under the stairs looked like it was swinging open all by itself. Then I realized it *was* swinging open but not by itself. Lacey was swinging it open. And she wasn't by herself either. She was with Kip.

And he had a pistol in her back!

CHAPTER ELEVEN

WHEN I saw Kip standing there with a crazy, drunken grin on his face and a pistol in his hand and realized that he and Lacey had been in the closet the whole time and heard everything that was said, I figured that the Lord was at last demanding payment in full for my sins. And, while I supposed it wasn't anything but right, the thought did pass through my mind that He was sort of overdoing it. Kip finding out about me having relations with his wife was bad enough. Catching me pinned under his practically naked eighteen-year-old sister just didn't seem real necessary.

I didn't know what to do so I just lay there letting Pert kiss me and trying to tuck as many of my vital parts under her as I could. I figured that he wouldn't shoot his own sister but if he saw any of me hanging out he might risk a shot at it. But then I rolled my eyes over at him again and saw that, although he was mighty drunk, it was cat-and-mouse whisky he had been drinking and he was going to toy with me a while before he killed me.

So, just as nice and gentlemanly as I could, I unscrewed my lips loose from Pert's and asked her if she would mind getting up off of me, please. She still didn't know that Kip and Lacey were standing there so she started snarling that I wasn't living up to our bargain.

"Buck Peters, I'd just as soon kiss a corpse. You promised you'd kiss me like you kissed Lacey!"

I shuddered and tried squirming back under her again and told her that she didn't understand. And she didn't. When she glared down at me and saw that my face was the color of a bowl of clabber, she thought that her love-making had nauseated me or something and despite her threat I was through with her. She started pleading with me.

"Buck, I'm just as much of a woman as Lacey is. You can do anything to me you did to her."

"Pert," I wheezed, "it ain't a matter of you being a woman, it's just a matter of your brother standing there with a gun that's got a barrel on it the size of a sewer!"

She turned real slow, saw Kip, boiled to her feet and showed what a sweet sensitive child she was.

"You bastard!" she spit at him. "You horrid, horrid bastard!"

I sighed and eased to my feet and took my first good look at Lacey to see how she was taking it. What I saw in her face made me want to weep. The Lord hadn't let me fall into the hands of one maniac, He had delivered me into the clutches of a whole covey of 'em.

Pert didn't seem to believe that Kip would shoot and Lacey seemed to believe it but didn't care if he did. She was standing there, her eyes all aglitter, looking a lot closer to laughing than to crying. Kip might kill her but he wasn't going to make her crawl. I realized then that if anybody came out of the mess alive it wouldn't be due to Pert or Lacey. It was up to me to soothe Kip until something could be worked out, so I tried.

"Kip," I said, "I'll bet I know what you're thinking, but you're wrong."

Of course, that wasn't much to say but it might have soothed him a little, if Lacey hadn't started laughing like it was the funniest thing she had ever heard. He shoved her out into the room and turned on me again.

"Take your damn clothes off!" he said. "You and Lacey both. You're going to bed."

"*Again?*" Lacey smirked.

"For the last damn time!" he said.

I had an idea of what was coming and so did Lacey, but Pert didn't want to believe it.

"Kip," she snapped, "just *what* do you think you're doing?"

He laughed real nasty. "What does a man usually do when he finds another man in bed with his wife?"

"In your case," Lacey said, "you ought to take notes!"

I shuddered and pleaded with her with my eyes to please stop goading him and give me a chance to think of something, but she just kept grinning and so did Pert. She asked him if he really expected her to believe that he was going to put me and Lacey in bed together and then just haul off and shoot us.

"You wouldn't shoot them any more than you shot Rita Singleton!" Pert sneered.

I thought that would get a few more of his hackles up but instead he looked real pleased about it.

"You don't think I killed Rita?" he said.

"You haven't got the nerve to kill anybody!"

"Then I'll count on you testifying to that," he said. "And then you testify that this psalm-singing sonofabitch was out in my back yard Saturday night laying my wife."

Pert looked as baffled as I felt. "You *are* drunk!" she said. "How could he have been in the back yard with your wife, when you say that your wife was in bed with you? There goes your alibi!"

"Who needs an alibi?" he said. "I'll tell the truth. I'll tell the jury that I was out drunk Saturday night and after I left Rita's I don't remember a thing. All I remembered was threatening to shoot her and after she got shot I got scared and lied about being in bed with my wife. Then I discovered I couldn't have been because she was out in the garden with Deacon Peters putting on a passion play for my eighteen-year-old sister."

Pert tried to laugh it off. "You're forgetting something. I've already said that *I* was that man in the garden."

He just grinned. "Not under oath you won't say it. You're going to tell the truth just like I'm going to tell it. You're going to tell the jury that I knew you were lying, that I sneaked out here thinking that I might find the man, whoever he was, out here with Lacey. I left my car in the bushes back a piece and came in here and made my dear wife confess to everything. Then we heard somebody coming and we hid in the closet and when I opened the door I'll be damned if there wasn't the passionate apostle of First Church again, and this time he's trying to outrage my little sister."

Pert shook her head. "And you think that will clear you?"

"Hell, yes, it will. What jury's gonna convict me? The bastard's nearly laid everything in my family but my mother and my cat and my mother's in Europe and the cat can climb trees."

Lacey started laughing again and he turned on her. "Laugh, damn it. It'll clear me of killing Rita, too. When Pert has to tell everybody about that jazz festival you and Buck staged in the garden Saturday night, it's gonna shock everybody so they won't know what to believe. If they were wrong about you and the Deacon, they could be wrong about me, and with nothing but circumstantial evidence against me that's all my lawyer is gonna need. Now keep taking those damn clothes off!"

With him waving that pistol like a drunk watering a lawn, there wasn't anything else to do. I started taking my shirt off and Lacey her blouse, with both of us trying to think of some flaw in his scheme.

Pert just stared at him. "You did kill Rita, didn't you?"

"Hell, yes, I killed her!" he said.

"How?" She still didn't want to believe it.

"Never mind how! And it won't do you any good telling a jury I admitted it. My lawyer will say you're trying to frame me for killing lover-boy. I don't want you on my side. The jury might think that *we* were trying to frame Buck."

He hadn't been drinking just cat-and-mouse whisky, he'd been drinking Ph.D. whisky. He had everything all thought out. And with a good lawyer and Sam and Phil and Chastain and them to help him out, he might just get away with three murders. Pert seemed to realize it too and started getting frantic.

"Kip, you can't do this. Buck didn't want to make love to me. I made him."

"And I made him too!" Lacey said. "He was under oath to do it."

I couldn't help blushing. They were trying to protect me with my own lie and for the first time I realized what a weak, bare-faced thing it was.

"Lacey didn't make me!" I told Kip. "I raped her when she wasn't but sixteen and she caught the habit. But she could have broken it, if it hadn't been for me, so I'm the only one you want to shoot."

He just grinned and said, "Why, Deacon, are you actually admitting that you like sex? Are you admitting that them love-feasts you've been holding in my back yard weren't just part of the Lord's work?"

I was admitting it. Not so much to him but to the Lord. I wanted His forgiveness for my sins and I knew now that my big-gest sin wasn't making love to Lacey or blackmailing people or plotting to legally kill Kip. Instead it was acting like it was the Lord's will that I do those things, just like Kip had said.

Way down deep I had known it wasn't so but a man can make himself believe anything, if he works at it hard enough, and I had been working at it ever since that day on the river bank. But I was going to reform. If the Lord would just deliver me and Lacey out of the mess we were in, I was going to change all my ways and never claim His sponsorship for my sinning again.

"Kip," I wheezed, "you can't kill Lacey. The jury still might not believe Pert's story about me and Lacey but if Lacey is there to tell it in person, they can't help believing it. She'll tell them such uncouth stories that you'll get a medal for killing me."

Lacey looked real touched at me trying to save her life but she had a funny way of showing her appreciation.

"Sure!" she smirked at Kip. "I'll tell them some uncouth stories. I'll tell them that this summer, when I wouldn't let you in my bedroom, which I never have done, you went down to your little sister's room and tried making love to her. You weren't that drunk, you bastard!"

That wiped the grin off his face. For a second, it looked like he was going to try and deny it but then he saw Pert glaring at him so he just started bellowing for us to hurry up and take our damn clothes off. I tried to keep him talking. I had to. We were about to run out of clothes to take off. Lacey was down to her pants and bra and I was down to my shorts.

"But, Kip," I said, "this ain't going to make you look too good. If you had shot us right off, a jury might say it was a heat of passion murder but if you strip us naked and put us in bed and *then* shoot us, it's ..."

"It's poetic justice. You two lived in bed, by God, you'll die in bed. Maybe I'll say that we found you this way, that Pert and I came out here to see Lacey and ..."

He kept on raving but I wasn't listening. All of a sudden I thought my poor, feverish mind had snapped and I was seeing things. I thought that out of the corner of my eye I had seen a face at the window behind him. Then I was positive of it. *There was somebody at the window.*

First, I saw the corner of this big, bald head come into view, then a lust-filled eye and then a big, drooling mouth. It was Mr. Johnson Phelps. For a second I wanted to kiss him, then I wanted to kill him.

There I was shaking in my shorts with a drunken maniac zeroed in on my navel with a gun but the old lecher was acting like I wasn't even there. All he was doing was licking his lips and gaping at Lacey. She had her hands up in back of her fumbling with the hooks on her bra. In another couple of seconds she would have it off. I had to do something quick. I not only didn't want the drooling old fool to see her that way, I was afraid, if he did, his blood pressure would shoot up so he'd have a stroke. And the way his eyes were popping out I wasn't sure that he wasn't already having one.

"Lacey," I said, "don't take that thing off!"

She stopped and stared at me. So did Kip.

"You want me to shoot you right now?" he snarled.

"You'd better!" I said. "Then you'd better shoot Mr. Johnson Phelps. He's looking in that window right behind you."

Mr. Phelps jerked his head back like he was already shot. Kip didn't make a move. He *knew* I was just trying to trick him into turning around so I could jump him. He leered at me and hollered over his shoulder, "Come on in, Phelps!"

Mr. Phelps wasn't about to come in. Instead a porch chair crashed through the window. Kip whirled and Pert made a grab for his gun. He flung her aside. I grabbed the gun with one hand and his throat with the other.

As I did, I heard this voice within me saying, "Kill him, Buck! Kill him!" I thought at first it was the voice of the Lord but then I remembered my promise not to put any more blame on Him. It was my own voice. I wanted to kill Kip and I was going to kill him. It wasn't Christian but it was legal. He was a self-confessed murderer and resisting the law.

I asked the Lord to forgive me and started twisting Kip's gun hand upward. He thought I was weakening but then he realized that the gun was twisting toward his head, not mine. Then the muzzle was against his head. He tried jerking away. I tightened my grip on his throat. The muzzle slid into his ear and hung. His eyes bugged out and he tried to gurgle something but I kept bringing the pressure to bear on his trigger finger. Then I heard a bone snap. Then an explosion. He went limp, his head fell back gushing blood and he was dead in my arms.

Pert started screaming and Lacey took her back to a bedroom. I let Kip slump to the floor. Mr. Phelps came in, all wildeyed and shaking.

"You bastard!" he snarled. "I heard you. You told him to shoot me!"

I ignored that and got a blanket out of the closet and covered Kip over. Mr. Phelps shook his head.

"Damn!" he wheezed. "I didn't know you were going to *kill* him!"

"It's just as well!" I said. "He confessed to killing Rita."

He gaped at me. "But he didn't kill Rita! He just *thought* he did. Weenie Thomas killed Rita!"

It was my turn to gape at him. "*Weenie* killed her?"

"Weenie's dead!" he said. "He came to at the hospital around one o'clock and must have wanted to die with a clear conscience. He told Delbert and Winston all about it. Twenty minutes later he was dead."

Naturally I couldn't believe it at first but Mr. Phelps kept talking and it all sounded real simple. He said that the way Weenie told it was that he had started out to Rita's himself around three o'clock Sunday morning. He had been doing some drunken brooding about that security warrant she had taken out against him and he wanted to tell her off. But, going out River Road, he had seen Kip Belton's car half in the ditch. Kip was slumped behind the wheel just about passed out and had a pistol in his lap and was mumbling something about shooting Rita.

With that Weenie had decided that he wouldn't only fix Rita for the warrant, he would get even with Kip for having made his sister commit suicide. So he had put Kip, who was practically unconscious, into the cab. Then he had gone out to Rita's, drug Kip down to her bedroom window, laid him on the ground, fired the shots through the window, shoved the pistol into Kip's hands and then taken off. But he hadn't meant to kill Rita. All he wanted to do was scare her and make Kip take the blame for all the disturbance.

The next morning, when he found out that he had accidentally killed her, he was scared to death that somebody might have seen him turning down her road. So, knowing that Kip wouldn't remember anything leading up to the shooting, he decided to frame him with the murder and came in and told me that drunk story of his. If anybody had seen him around Rita's, the story would take care of that.

And, to keep anybody from suspecting that he had framed Kip, he had hung the rap on him gradually instead of accusing him outright. He had rolled Kip for his money before taking him down to Rita's so it was real easy to plant the money clip in the back seat of his cab for Delbert to find.

Kip, he figured, would finally break down and confess that all he remembered was coming to under Rita's window with the pistol in his hand. And, by admitting that he was that drunk, he wouldn't be able to say that Weenie's story about the cab ride was a lie and he would be stuck with the murder. The fact that Sam and Phil had heard him threatening Rita was just so much gravy.

"So," Mr. Phelps wound up, "Weenie got that all off his chest and died and after the excitement was all over I got in my boat and headed up this way for my lodge. About a half mile from here my motor conked out and I came up here thinking I could borrow Lacey's. *Now,* you tell me something."

I was still so intrigued with Kip and Weenie that I didn't realize what he was driving at.

"Well, it all fits," I said. "Kip couldn't tell Pert any of the details of the murder so Weenie had him figured right. All he remembered was coming to under the window. He probably headed home on foot, saw his car in the ditch, got in it and …"

Mr. Phelps didn't let me finish. "That's not what I want you to tell me!" he sneered. "What I want you to tell me is just what the hell was going on in this room when I got here. I saw your car and figured I'd find a prayer meeting but instead it looked like a holdup in a whorehouse. You in your drawers, and Lacey and Pert in their ..."

In all the excitement, I had forgot about that. I still hadn't won my fight to save mine and Lacey's names.

"Well, Mr. Phelps," I drawled, picking up my undershirt, "I'll tell you. I ..."

"No, *I'll* tell *you!*" he gloated. "*You* were the man that Stool saw in the garden. You came out here to tell Lacey what had happened and then you decided to have a little quickie and, right in the middle of it, Kip walked in and ..."

"Mr. Phelps," I interrupted, "don't you think it could have happened like this instead? Pert was the man in the garden but I brought her out here to check her story with Lacey. Kip, though, had come out ahead of us to see Lacey. She was out on the river, though, and while he was waiting on her he got so remorseful, thinking that he was Rita's murderer, that he committed suicide and Pert and I found his body when we came in!"

He just kept grinning.

"Mr. Phelps," I said, "you think you got me, don't you?"

"Right down to the sheet burns on your knees!" he said. "You didn't get them kneeling in prayer. Hell, yes, I got you!"

"Well," I said, "if you were on your way up to your lodge just to go fishing, then maybe you have got me."

"Now just what the hell is that supposed to mean?" he said, trying to look real offended.

"Just this," I said. "We'll get in my car and go back to town and you tell everybody that Kip caught Deacon Buckingham Peters and Lacey Belton, the Sunday School teacher, in bed together. You tell them that and see how many believe you and then I'll go out to your house and see if your wife will believe what I tell her. I'll tell her that there's a blonde waiting for you at your lodge and I can take her up there and ..."

He drowned me out. "All right, damn it, it was suicide! When I got here you were in full uniform chanting the Twenty-Third Psalm over his remains. Does that suit you?"

For the first time in my life I was blackmailing somebody and not blaming it on the Lord and I felt a whole lot better about it. It was going to be a whole lot easier begging His forgiveness than it had been taking over His job and granting myself forgiveness.

"And, Mr. Phelps," I said, "don't you think that our coroner, Dr. Winston, will think that it's suicide too?"

"I wouldn't be surprised," he sighed.

"And don't you think," I said, "that a coroner's jury composed of you and Sam Bates and Phil Gaunt and Clyde Mansfield and Rupe Hobson will back him up?"

"Yes, you fiendish sonofabitch, we just might!"

And that's the way it happened and everybody seemed mighty relieved to have everything all settled so nicely. Lacey and I are married now and mighty happy, especially since Pert let it be known around town that Lacey had never been anything to Kip but a wife in name only. I'm still reformed and an elder in the church which makes Mama and her friends mighty happy. I'm also running the Belton plant—now, Satter-field-Belton—and thinking about running for Mayor. Mr. Phelps is telling everybody that I'm the only man with the virtues necessary for taking his place.

As for Delbert, he is Chief of Police and running a mighty well-disciplined town. Mainly because he keeps the rumor going that I left him Rita's diary. As for Pert, she is making her home with us, she and Lacey being real good friends...except, of course, when Pert asks me to show her the garden. She's just kidding, though. The only thing exciting that happens back there now is church picnics!

www.ingramcontent.com/pod-product-compliance
Lightning Source LLC
Chambersburg PA
CBHW020656260626
47157CB00008B/3053